THE ORIGINS OF LIFE

THE WORLD OF SCIENCE LIBRARY
GENERAL EDITOR: ROBIN CLARKE

THE ORIGINS OF LIFE

Cyril Ponnamperuma

E. P. DUTTON   NEW YORK

To Valli

First published in the U.S.A. 1972 by E. P. Dutton & Co., Inc
Copyright 1972 in London, England, by Thames and Hudson Ltd
All rights reserved.
First Edition
Printed in the Netherlands.

Library of Congress Catalog Card Number: 72-183747
SBN Number: 0-525-17195-9 Clothbound
0-525-04125-7 Paperback

577
p

CONTENTS

PREFACE

'Even the formulation of this problem is beyond the reach of any one scientist, for such a scientist would have to be at the same time a competent mathematician, physicist, and experienced organic chemist, he should have a very extensive knowledge of geology, geophysics, and geochemistry and, besides all this, be absolutely at home in all biological disciplines.' Thus spoke J. D. Bernal on the origin of life, a quarter century ago, in the thirty-first Guthrie lecture to the British Physical Society. Along with the question of the origin of the universe and the origin of intelligence, the problem of life's beginning ranks as one of the most fundamental of all science.

It is with a feeling of awe and inadequacy that we approach the task of proposing in scientific terms the sequence of events in the universe which culminated in the appearance of life. Chemical studies have proved to be one of the most fruitful avenues to our understanding of the transition from the non-living to the living. The successful simulation of the pre-biotic milieu, and the identification of the building blocks of life in a 'primordial broth' which is presumed to have constituted the oceans of the juvenile earth, have led us to believe that we have a firm handle to unravel this enigma. The discovery of amino acids in extraterrestrial samples, such as meteorites, has given us some measure of conviction that many of the processes we outlined for the infant earth are commonplace in the universe. They constitute a part of the orderly sequence of cosmic evolution. While buoyed by these staggering discoveries, we must introduce an element of cautious restraint into our optimism that a solution is near at hand. The laborious transcribing of the alphabet of life is only a rudimentary first step in the birth of nature's masterpiece.

With the dawn of the space age, the public awareness of and interest in the question of life's origins has rocketed to new heights. If we discover life on Mars, and can establish, with certainty, that the Martian biota is different from its terrestrial counterpart, there would be new evidence to bolster our thesis of chemical evolution. Arising twice in a single planetary system, life must occur abundantly elsewhere in the enormous number of planetary systems.

A chemist by training and occupation, I have emphasized the chemical aspects of the problem. There are inherent weaknesses in reliance on experiment alone, yet the results have been most rewarding. Although the book is intended for the non-specialist, I have journeyed freely into the world of chemical formulae and pathways of chemical reactions, to dramatize a molecular solution to the greatest mystery of all time.

To Mr Stephen England, of Thames and Hudson, I am deeply indebted for assembling a magnificent array of pictures to complement my story. His unflagging attention to every sophisticated detail in the genesis of this book is gratefully acknowledged.

Cyril Ponnamperuma
University of Maryland, 1972

How life began is a question that has mystified man ever since he appeared upon this earth. The modern scientist recognizes an evolutionary pattern in nature. His knowledge of cosmological discoveries leads him to the assumption that life is the outcome of natural processes in the universe. He is optimistic that the results of laboratory investigations will furnish a solution to this ultimate mystery. The idea of the biological unity of everything living and the evolution of the higher forms of life from the lower, a concept which caused a revolt among the thinkers of the nineteenth century, is today the cornerstone of modern biology. If this theory is drawn to its logical conclusion, another form of evolution has to be postulated prior to Darwinian evolution, namely, chemical evolution.

Chemical evolution connotes all that occurred before the emergence of life. In 1871, the British physicist Tyndall, in his *Fragments of Science for Unscientific People*, dramatically highlighted this question: 'Darwin placed at the root of life a primordial germ, from which he conceived that the amazing richness and variety of the life now upon the earth's surface might be deduced. If this hypothesis were true, it would not be final. The

How life began has been the subject of speculation and mythology from the dawn of history. Opposite: the Hindu legend has good and evil spirits pulling alternately on the body of a snake to rotate the sacred mountain Mandara to and fro as it stands on the back of the tortoise, Vishnu. The result is the churning of the ocean – the cradle of all living matter

human imagination would infallibly look behind the germ and, however hopeless the attempt, would enquire into the history of its genesis . . . A desire immediately arises to connect the present life of our planet with the past. We wish to know something of our remotest ancestry . . . Does life belong to what we call matter or is it an independent principle inserted into matter at some suitable epoch, when the physical conditions became such as to permit of the development of life?'

The problem before us is a complex one. Life today is the result of the intertwining of an intricate series of events over billions of years. The difficulty is to unravel the tangled skein. According to Bergson, 'the evolution movement would be a simple one, and we should soon be able to determine its direction if life had described a single course like that of a solid ball shot from a cannon. But it proceeds rather like a shell, which suddenly bursts into fragments, which fragments, being

'*Let there be lights in the firmament of the heaven. . . . Let the waters bring forth abundantly the moving creature that hath life.*' *The famous mosaic in the Cathedral of Monreale, Italy, tells the Biblical story of the Creation*

themselves shells, burst in their turn into fragments, destined to burst again, and so on for a time incommensurably long. We perceive only what is nearest to us, namely, the scattered movements of the pulverized explosions. From them we have to go back, stage by stage, to the original movement.'

Several theories have been propounded through the ages to explain the beginnings of life. Awed by the mystery of the world around him, man has invoked the concept of special creation. To a supernatural being, and to an omnipotent power, he has attributed everything that he sees around him, including life itself. The account of creation in the first chapter of Genesis is part of the western heritage. Similar descriptions are found in the sacred books of other religions. Although metaphorical rather than literal in nature, these explanations of the stages in cosmic creation have largely contributed to the fact that the study of the origin of life, until recently, has been relegated to the realm of metaphysics and philosophy. Today, this subject has assumed its proper place within the domain of scientific enquiry. There is no attempt to prove or to disprove any belief but, rather, an endeavour to solve a cosmic enigma.

Among other theories is the one attributed to Arrhenius, who suggested that the seeds of life may have come to us from another planet. This is the theory of panspermia, according to which spores may have been blown by the power of solar radiation through the vacuum of space till they reached a fertile haven where they sprang to life again. They may have been carried on meteorites, or dust particles, which travel at enormous speeds through the vast and empty reaches of the universe. It is highly improbable that microorganisms could travel such boundless distances, be exposed to ultraviolet light, and still survive without adequate

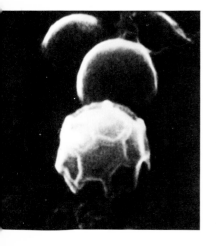

This electron micrograph shows, magnified 20,000 times, a sugar-mould spore of a kind that could, in theory, be blown through space by radiation pressure, to spread life from one planet to another. To spread, not to create: the 'panspermia' theory only pushes the problem one step further back

protection. Were a cosmic spore to overcome the hazards of such a journey, this theory of panspermia only removes the problem one stage further. It still leaves unanswered the question of how life began on the other planetary body from which the spores emigrated.

Spontaneous generation

For centuries, the idea of spontaneous generation had been regarded as an acceptable explanation for the origin of life. Mistaken interpretation of the evidence of the senses led many to believe that life arose from non-life, in the grossest possible sense. Worms were observed in mud, maggots were seen in decaying meat, and mice were found in old linen. It was believed, therefore, that these living things arose from the non-living host in which they were found. Among the first to propose such a hypothesis was the Greek philosopher Aristotle. In his *Metaphysics* he suggested spontaneous genera-tion as a reasonable explanation for the origin of life. He cited the example of fireflies arising from morning dew. Before Aristotle, Anaximander had

Microscopic fungus found in sup-posedly sterile broth, put forward by the nineteenth-century scientist Bastian as evidence of spontaneous generation

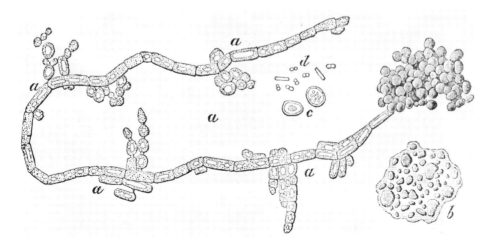

Francesco Redi: burgeoning scientific method

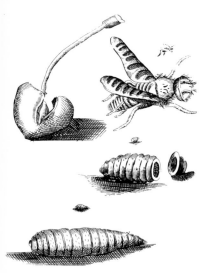

How did the fly get into the cherry? The problem led Redi to his disproof of spontaneous generation

described how the first animals arose from sea slime, and how men came from the bellies of fish. The long line of western thinkers – Newton, Harvey, Descartes, Van Helmont, among others – accepted this theory without question. Christian philosophers quoted scripture in support of spontaneous generation. According to the first chapter of Genesis, they argued, God did not create plants and animals directly, but bade the waters to bring them forth. We have similar statements in the ancient philosophical writings of the East. The sacred books of the Rig Veda refer to the beginning of life from the primary elements. The Atharva Veda postulates the oceans as the cradle of all living matter.

References to these beliefs abound in the world's literature. In the *Georgics*, Virgil describes how a swarm of bees arose from the carcass of a calf. Lucretius, in *De Rerum Natura*, refers to the earth as the mother of all living things:

> With right
> It followeth then that earth has won the name
> Of Mother, since from earth have all things sprung.
> And even now we see full many a breed
> Of living creatures rise out of the earth
> Begot by rains and by the genial warmth
> The sun doth shed.

In *Antony and Cleopatra*, Lepidus tells Mark Antony, 'Your serpent of Egypt is bred now of your mud by the operation of your sun: so is your crocodile.'

Such ideas, however, could not long withstand the rigorous scrutiny of burgeoning scientific method. Francesco Redi, a celebrated member of the Accademia del Cimento, demonstrated that the worms in meat were larvae from the eggs of flies. His proofs were as simple as they were decisive. He showed that meat placed under a screen of muslin so

that flies could not lay their eggs on it never developed maggots.

Despite these conclusive results, the debate on the origin of life continued to rage for it was about this time that Antony van Leeuwenhoek invented the microscope. A whole new world of minute creatures was now revealed to man's eyes. Those who looked through the microscope wondered about the origin of these new forms. They were unable to discern anything that resembled the process of sexual generation and were led to believe that the microorganisms were spontaneously

Antony van Leeuwenhoek, pioneer microscopist, stands to the left of the lecturer in Cornelis de Man's painting 'The Anatomy Lesson'

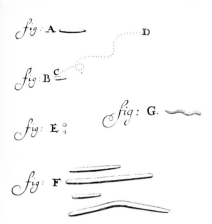

'Living animalcules, very prettily a-moving' was how Leeuwenhoek described these bacteria taken from his saliva, seen under his newly invented microscope

formed from the non-living materials present in the mixtures.

This recipe for mice, given by the Belgian physician and chemist Van Helmont, epitomizes the conviction with which the doctrine of spontaneous generation was adhered to by its proponents. 'If a dirty undergarment is squeezed into the mouth of a vessel containing wheat, within a few days, (say 21), a ferment drained from the garments and transformed by the smell of the grain, encrusts the wheat itself with its own skin and turns it into mice . . . And, what is more remarkable, the mice from corn and undergarments are neither weanlings or sucklings nor premature but they jump out fully formed.'

Jean Baptiste van Helmont

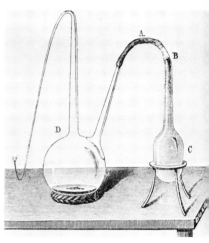

Those who supported the idea of spontaneous generation continued to perform poorly conceived experiments in an attempt to produce new and more evidence in aid of the concept.

About this time, the French Academy offered a prize to anyone who would once and for all scotch the controversy which had vexed the entire scientific world. Louis Pasteur conducted a series of carefully designed investigations. His swan-necked flasks are now symbolic of the research which sounded the death knell of the theory of spontaneous generation. He had first proved that air did

Above, left: Louis Pasteur lecturing. He finally scotched the theory of spontaneous generation with the aid of his swan-necked flasks, some of which can be seen (above) on the table beside him

A corner of Pasteur's laboratory. The great scientist himself is portrayed fondling two of his experimental animals, in a cartoon from Vanity Fair, 1875

contain microscopically observable organized bodies. He aspirated large quantities of air through a tube containing a plug of cotton and, when the cotton was dissolved in a mixture of alcohol and ether and the sediment examined microscopically, there were, in addition to inorganic matter, large numbers of small round bodies which were indistinguishable from microorganisms. Pasteur also observed that if air was heated and then introduced into a boiled infusion, there was no evidence of microbial development. His critics objected that the vital principle had been destroyed in this process. To counteract this unexpected opposition, new experiments were designed. The swan-necked flasks were open to the atmosphere, but the dips and curves trapped the incoming microbes and the solution in the flask remained clear. It was only when the neck of one of the flasks was broken that the invading microbes turned the solution murky. If the microorganisms did not enter the flask, there was no evidence of life in the solution.

Although Pasteur's work clearly demonstrated that it was futile to subscribe to the theory of spontaneous generation in the form in which scientists of the nineteenth century knew it, this was not the end of the story. Across the Channel, there were still those who clung to the thesis. Tyndall, who was a fervent supporter of Pasteur, undertook to refute many ideas which were still in vogue among scientists in England. It was in the course of these experiments that he hit upon the process which is now described as 'Tyndallization', in which discontinuous heating was developed as an extremely valuable method of sterilization. Pasteur had dealt only with common microbes that could enter his solutions from the atmosphere. However, this method of sterilization could not have killed spores. It was only the repeated boiling, for brief periods of

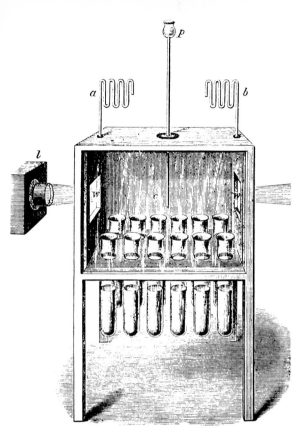

Apparatus used by Tyndall to study putrefaction. From his work came the discontinuous-heating method of sterilization still known as Tyndallization

time, that helped to destroy them. Although resistant to boiling, they are susceptible to sterilization by heat when allowed to germinate. While Pasteur's feat has been acclaimed as having delivered the *coup de grâce* to the doctrine of spontaneous generation, Tyndall's research further bolstered Pasteur's work. In 1864, Pasteur announced his results before the French Academy with the words, 'Never will the doctrine of spontaneous generation arise from this mortal blow.' It is, perhaps, ironic that we tell beginning students in biology about Pasteur's experiments as the triumph of reason over mysticism yet we are coming back to spontaneous generation, albeit in a more refined and scientific sense, namely, to chemical evolution.

CHEMICAL EVOLUTION

According to the hypothesis of chemical evolution, life arose from non-life. In this scheme of things, life is regarded as a result of the development of matter. It is a property which had not existed earlier and which arose at a particular point in the history of our planet. The origin of life is an occurrence which may not be ascribed to some definite place or time; rather, it was the result of a gradual process operating on the earth over an inconceivably long span of time. It was a process of evolution and maturation which spread over millions of years, and reached its zenith in the biosphere of today. This progression may be described as taking place in distinct and successive phases: from the inorganic to the organic, and from the organic to the biological.

Among one of the first to consider the problem from the scientific point of view was Charles Darwin. His now celebrated letter to his friend Hooker formulates how 'in some warm little pond, with all sorts of ammonia and phosphoric salts, light, heat, electricity, etc., present . . . a protein compound was chemically formed ready to undergo still more complex changes'. This idea contains the germ of Darwin's philosophy on the origin of life. His own thought was, perhaps, influenced by

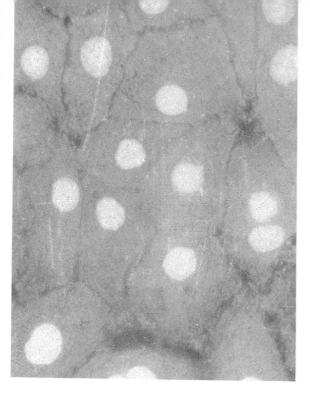

Nucleic acids, the 'blueprints' and 'templates' of protein synthesis, are shown up in this photomicrograph (× 3,500) of human cells. Special staining makes the DNA, in the nuclei, show up as white spots, while the RNA is the greyish background seen throughout the cell fluid

Below: Charles Darwin, whose ideas on how life began, 'in some warm little pond', were years in advance of his time

that of his grandfather, Erasmus Darwin. It was in his *Temple of Nature* that Erasmus Darwin had written, 'all vegetables and animals now existing were originally derived from the smallest microscopic ones formed by spontaneous vitality.'

After Darwin, Tyndall, who, as we have already seen, was active in experimental work related to spontaneous generation, had suggested that if every portion of a living organism could be reduced to inorganic matter, the reverse, from the inorganic to the organic, should also be possible. According to him, special arrangements of elements in living bodies led to the phenomena that we describe as life. In 1868, Thomas Huxley, speaking in Edinburgh before the British Association for the Advancement of Science at its annual meeting in a lecture entitled 'The Physical Basis of Life', inferred that protoplasm was substantially the same over the whole range of living things. To Huxley, the existence of life depended on certain molecules such as carbonic acid, water, and nitrogenous compounds. These compounds, the building blocks of life, were lifeless in themselves but, when brought together, gave rise to protoplasm.

For over half a century after Huxley, there appeared to be little or no interest in the problem of the origin of life. No one dared to speculate in public for, after all, Pasteur had demonstrated that spontaneous generation could not take place. No self-respecting scientist would spend his time trying to prove something which a man as renowned and esteemed for his scientific contributions as Louis Pasteur had disproved. The advancement of science in one area of study sometimes has a constraining effect on the progress of knowledge in another field.

In 1924, the Russian biochemist Alexander Ivanovich Oparin published a preliminary booklet stating that 'there is no fundamental difference between a living organism and lifeless matter. The complex combination of manifestations and properties so characteristic of life must have arisen in the process of the evolution of matter.' This treatise was translated into English for the first time in 1938. He described how

at first there were the simple solutions of organic substances, the behaviour of which was governed by the properties of their component atoms and the arrangement of those atoms in the molecular structure. But gradually, as the result of growth and increased complexity of the molecules, new properties have come into being and a new colloidal-chemical order was imposed on the more simple organic chemical relations. These newer properties were determined by the spatial

A. I. Oparin, father of modern studies on the origins of life

arrangement and mutual relationship of the molecules. . . . In this process biological orderliness already comes into prominence. Competitive speed of growth, struggle for existence and, finally, natural selection determined such a form of material organization which is characteristic of living things of the present time.

In 1928, the British biologist Haldane, independently of Oparin, published a paper in the *Rationalist Annual* in which he speculated on the early conditions which may have been suitable for the emergence of terrestrial life. He considered ultraviolet light from the sun to be of paramount importance. When this source of energy acted upon the earth's primitive atmosphere, a vast array of organic compounds was formed. Among these may have occurred sugars and some of the amino acids necessary for proteins. Haldane postulated that these compounds accumulated in the primitive oceans till they had the consistency of 'a hot dilute soup'. It is in this primordial broth that life probably began.

J. B. S. Haldane, to whom is due the concept of the 'primordial soup'

Another landmark in the historical and scientific development of the subject was the classic paper presented by J. D. Bernal of the University of London before the British Physical Society in 1947, entitled 'The Physical Basis of Life'. The oceans of organic compounds, Bernal theorized, must have been dilute in composition. Some simple and natural machinery was required to produce the concentrations necessary for the condensation of small molecules into the polymers and macromolecules necessary for life. The lagoons and pools along the oceans may have played a vital role in such processes. The adsorption of organic compounds by fine clay deposits, both marine and freshwater, must have been extremely fruitful in

J. D. Bernal proposed a way in which dilute solutions of compounds could have been concentrated to give rise to the larger molecules needed for life

25

promoting the condensations necessary for the origin of macromolecules. Photochemical products may have been adsorbed by these surfaces. Clay may have performed several functions: the adsorption of the molecules, the joining of them together, and the means of protecting the molecules from the lethal ultraviolet rays of the sun.

Possible planets

These ideas on chemical evolution, implicit in the writings of Bernal, Haldane and Oparin, are based on a number of fundamental considerations. Of basic importance are the astronomical discoveries of the twentieth century. There was a time when it was believed that planetary systems were rather rare in the universe. The material ejected from the close encounter between the sun and another star was thought to have condensed into the planets and their satellites. An alternative theory links the origin of our solar system with the explosion of a star as it passed near the sun. However, such tidal theories are discounted by modern astronomers.

It is generally held that planets are plentiful in the universe. Each one of the stars visible in the sky is like our sun. Powerful telescopes have revealed the presence of more than 10^{20} (one hundred million million million) of these stars. Therefore, there is nothing unique about our sun, which is the mainstay of life upon this earth. If the laws of chemistry and physics are universal in character, the same sequence of events should occur elsewhere in the universe.

There must be more than 10^{20} opportunities for the existence of life in the cosmos. However, not all these stars can have planetary systems. A double star for example, one star moving around another, is a case in point. A planet has also to be a certain distance from the sun in order to have the conditions

Opposite: the 'Whirlpool' nebula. Itself made up of millions upon millions of stars, it is only one of a hundred thousand million nebulae in the observable universe. How many of these stars have planets like ours?

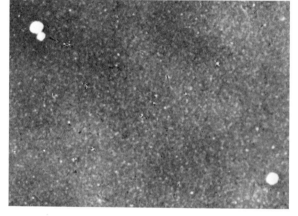

The double star Krueger 60, in the constellation Cepheus, is the closest known double to the sun (about 14 light-years distant). Double systems like this could not retain planets

necessary for life. In our solar system, Mercury is too close to the sun, and too hot, to have the material and conditions required for living organisms. Pluto is perhaps too cold, and the reactions leading to the formation of organic compounds may not have taken place at very low temperatures. A planet has also to be of the right size to hold an atmosphere. Gravitational force is required to prevent the escape of the lighter gases which are necessary for biological processes to take place, and to retain the water which is essential for life. The moon, for example, is too small a body to hold an atmosphere. On the other hand, a planet such as Mars, or Venus, is big enough. In our planetary system, seven out of the nine planets can sustain an atmosphere. Further, one might consider that a planet requires certain indispensable chemicals in its atmosphere. These restrictions – distance from the sun, size of the planetary body, and chemical composition – would reduce the number of possible sites for life beyond the earth. The astronomer Harlow Shapley took all these considerations into account and estimated that there are a hundred million such possibilities. Today, Shapley's calculations are considered to be rather conservative.

Other cosmologists have examined several factors related to the origin of planetary systems. They have contemplated the evolution of stars, galaxies, planetary systems, atmospheres, and the lifetimes of biological systems, and concluded that about 5 per cent of all stars should be able to support life. This gives us a figure of 10^{18} possibilities for the existence of life in the universe.

Taking into account the relationship between the chemical composition of the planets and that of a main sequence star, Harrison Brown has suggested that there may be some sixty objects more massive than Mars in the neighbourhood of visible stars. Stars, together with cold objects, may occur in clusters, random in size. On this basis, practically every star should have a planetary system associated with it. In our galaxy alone, there must be at least a hundred thousand million planetary systems.

Our ideas on the existence of planetary systems are intimately connected with the concepts related to their origin. As far back as 1755, Kant had suggested that the planets arose from the condensation of a diffuse and tenuous mass of gas and dust, by a

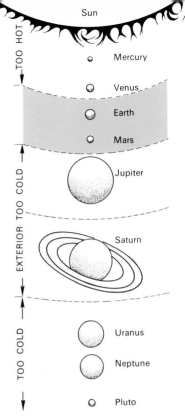

In the solar system can be seen the narrow range of conditions outside of which living organisms could not develop. Jupiter, though externally cold, has internal conditions suitable for the evolution of life

From the spectrum of a star its chemical composition can be deduced, and thus the chemistry of any planets it may have

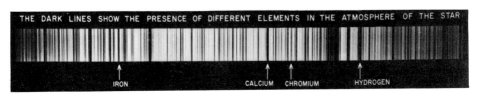

THE DARK LINES SHOW THE PRESENCE OF DIFFERENT ELEMENTS IN THE ATMOSPHERE OF THE STAR

IRON   CALCIUM   CHROMIUM   HYDROGEN

The gaseous nebula M8 in Sagittarius. Dark dots (arrowed) are clouds of gas and dust – each at least as big as the solar system – where stars may be forming

slow process of accretion. The remainder of this early nebula condensed to form the sun. This nebular hypothesis of Kant was independently put forward by the astronomer Laplace. This concept held sway until about 1900 when it was seriously challenged by Chamberlin, Moulton, and Jeans.

Several rival arguments were advanced, particularly tidal theories which suggested some form of close encounter between a sun and another star. An ejection of solar material was considered to have given rise to our planets. However, it soon became clear to most astronomers that the processes of planetary formation were closely connected with those of star formation. According to current astronomical thinking, the solar system may have begun its life in the embryonic cloud of gas which was held together by the force of its own gravity. The dense centre of this cloud must have shrunk approximately to the size of the present sun. The cooler and less dense regions surrounding the primitive sun must have developed, under the force of gravity, to give rise to the planets. It is generally accepted by astronomers that the planets in the universe suitable for life are of common occurrence. The conditions in which life could begin, and evolve, and survive, are no longer considered to be unique.

The Weizsäcker theory of how the planets could have condensed out of a cloud of gas surrounding the primitive sun. Turbulence in the rotating dish-shaped cloud forms a series of concentric rings, within which eddies are set up. Where two eddies come into contact, planets start to condense, the process speeded by the increasing force of their own gravity

Astronomical observations have also shown that seven out of the nearest hundred stars may have planetary systems around them. Although planets cannot be observed directly, aberrations in the movement of these stars seem to suggest that they have planets in orbit around them whose gravitational forces give rise to the observed fluctuations. A well-known example is Barnard's Star, which has been observed over long periods of time by the astronomer Van de Kamp. He concluded that there must be a planet orbiting round it, at least as big as Jupiter.

All these considerations have led students of the origin of life to believe that life must be common in the universe, and not unique to this earth. In searching for a solution to this problem we are concerned with the entire universe. The earth becomes a model laboratory for what may have happened on innumerable occasions in other solar systems.

It is remarkable that this conclusion, which present-day astronomers have obtained by the meticulous analysis of precise scientific data, was prophetically described by the Italian Giordano Bruno in the sixteenth century.

Sky, universe, all-embracing ether, and immeasurable space alive with movement . . . all these are of one nature. In space there are countless constellations, suns and planets; we see only the suns because they give light; the planets remain invisible, for they are small and dark. There are also numberless earths circling around their suns, no worse and no less inhabited than this globe of ours. For no reasonable mind can assume that heavenly bodies which may be far more magnificent than ours would not bear upon them creatures similar or even superior to those upon our human Earth.

The basic molecules

We now turn from astronomy to biochemistry. Modern biochemical discoveries have underlined the remarkable unity of living matter. In all organisms, from the minutest microbe to the largest mammal, there appear to be two basic molecules which interact to give us the phenomenon that we describe as life. These two molecules are nucleic acid and protein, which together provide the foundation for all life.

These molecules are complex in form, and have very large molecular weights. The nucleic acid

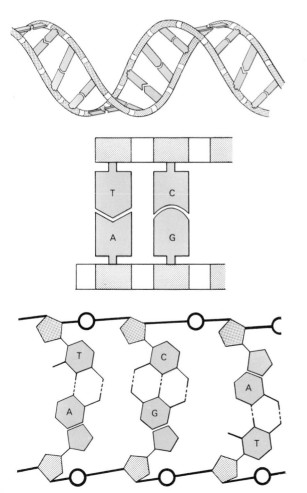

Nucleic acid, present in the nucleus of every living cell, is a large and complex molecule. It has to be, for it is a 'blueprint' carrying more information than any made by man. It is shaped like a spiral staircase (left), the sides being alternately phosphates and sugars and the 'treads' being nitrogen-containing molecules called bases. A closer look at the 'treads' of the staircase (centre) shows that each one is a pair of bases, one fitting into the other like a hand into a glove. One of each pair is a 'purine ring', a pentagon attached to a hexagon, while the other is a 'pyrimidine', a simple six-sided molecule. Purine will not pair with purine, nor pyrimidine with pyrimidine; thus thymine (T) will join only to adenine (A), cytosine (C) only to guanine (G). This specific pairing (below) is the code in which the cellular blueprint of life is written

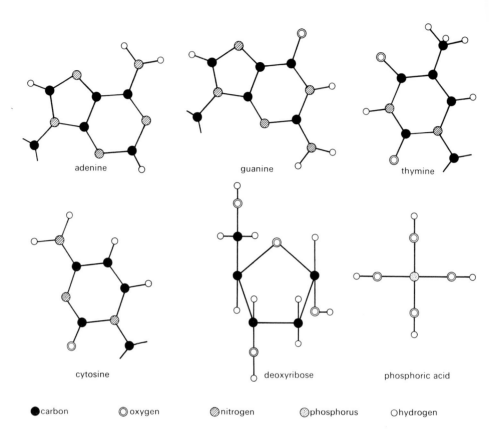

adenine   guanine   thymine

cytosine   deoxyribose   phosphoric acid

● carbon   ◎ oxygen   ⊘ nitrogen   ⊛ phosphorus   ○ hydrogen

The detailed structure of the three parts – bases, phosphate, sugar – of the DNA molecule is shown above

molecules, DNA (deoxyribose nucleic acid) and RNA (ribose nucleic acid), consist of *nucleotides,* which are the single links in the nucleic acid chain. A nucleotide, in turn, is made up of a sugar, a base, and a phosphate. In the case of DNA, the bases are adenine, guanine, cytosine and thymine. In RNA, the cytosine is replaced by uracil, and the sugar, deoxyribose, of DNA appears as ribose in RNA. Adenine and guanine are purines, and are structurally made up of a five-membered ring built on the side of a six-sided molecule. The pyrimidines, cytosine, thymine, and uracil, consist only of the six-membered ring. The purines are paired with the pyrimidines by an electrostatic effect called hydrogen bonding.

The DNA molecule itself is a helix which resembles a coiled ladder. The coils are tight, and billions of them are packed into a single cell. The rungs of the ladder are the base pairs. It is this arrangement of the ladder, with infinite possibilities of permutations and combinations, which gives rise to the variety that we know in life today. Not only is this molecule the chief controller of the cell's activities, but it also directs the synthesis of other molecules, particularly proteins.

The protein molecule, too, is very large in molecular weight, and is composed of twenty different amino acids. Of these, aspartic acid and

Amino acids, joined end to end like poppet beads or railroad trucks, form a protein molecule. With twenty different amino acids, the permutations are infinite and the protein molecule can be a large one. This model of the myoglobin molecule – magnified in scale 125 million times – was one of the first for which the arrangement and folding (characteristic and unvarying) was worked out in detail

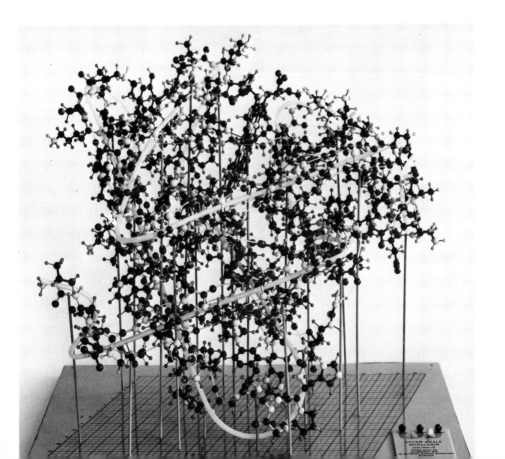

glutamic acid are acidic in nature. Lysine and arginine are basic. The rest are considered neutral since their acidic and basic ends are equally balanced. They are able to join together to form chains with the aid of peptide linkages.

The alphabet of life thus appears to be a simple one – twenty amino acids, five bases, two sugars, and one phosphate in every living organism on earth. Although there may be variations in the structure of nucleic acids or the form of proteins, the presence of the same small numbers of molecules in all living organisms must, of necessity, lead us to the conclusion that all life must have had one single genesis.

Not only does one see this kinship in the constituents of living organisms, but also in the manner in which metabolic processes take place. It is perhaps no exaggeration to say that there is a remarkable uniformity about these processes throughout the entire biosphere. The cycles of change from food to energy appear to have extremely consistent and similar lines, whether in mammal or microbe. Molecular and functional identity strongly argue a single chemical origin.

This great similarity which is seen among living organisms, whether in the smallest microbe or the most advanced intelligent human being, can also be extended to the early chemical world. Some of the processes that are evident in biology may be considered to be a recapitulation of what may have taken place in prebiology. The evidence available from practically every field of science suggests that there is a unity in nature. We have divided this into categories for human convenience. The division of matter into living and non-living is, perhaps an arbitrary one. It is a convenient method of distinguishing, for instance, a man from a rock. We have no difficulty in saying that one is living and that the other is not. However, when we deal with virus particles and the small organisms, this description appears to be totally inappropriate and unsatisfactory.

Over thirty years ago, Wendell Stanley separated and crystallized the tobacco mosaic virus from the leaves of the tobacco plant. On his laboratory shelf, there were crystals of the tobacco mosaic virus.

Dr Heinz L. Fraenkel-Conrat (left) and the late Dr Wendell Stanley examining tobacco plants infected with tobacco mosaic virus. The electron microscope shows the virus (below) as a rod-like particle with a regularly coiled protein coat (cross-section, below left) and a thread of DNA down the centre. Crystals of this virus stay inert for years in a jar on the laboratory shelf; placed on a tobacco leaf, they infect it like a living pest. So how does one define 'living'?

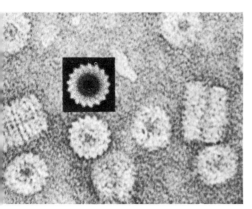

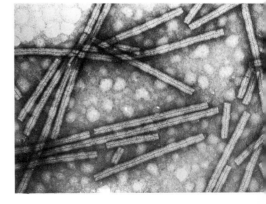

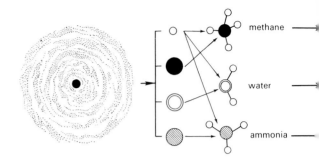

Occasionally, he would take a few crystals of this virus and place them on a tobacco leaf. The leaves would become infected. Such experiments, and subsequent reconstruction of this virus by other collaborators of Stanley – Fraenkel-Conrat and Robley Williams – underlined the need to define the words 'life' and 'living'. The tobacco mosaic virus was taken apart, and the protein of one virus was coupled with the nucleic acid of another. The reconstituted virus particles were still infective. At least in one case we see that it was hard to define where life began, which was living and which was not living.

Such considerations led the British biochemist Norman W. Pirie to write his very expressive essay entitled 'The Meaninglessness of the Terms "Life" and "Living"'. He compared the use of the terms 'living' and 'non-living' to 'acid' and 'base' as used in chemistry. While sodium hydroxide is distinctly alkaline, and sulphuric acid a powerful acid, in between there is a whole variation in strength. Water, for example, is halfway between, and is neither acidic nor basic. The chemist has overcome the confusion arising from the use of these two terms by inventing a new nomenclature. He is thus able to describe all the observed phenomena in terms of one quantity – hydrogen ion concentration.

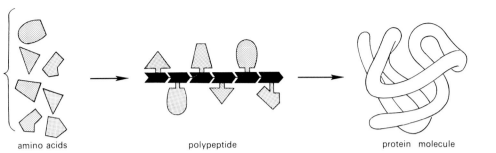

amino acids   polypeptide   protein molecule

Thus, a liquid may have a hydrogen ion concentration of 10^{-4} or of 10^{-8}, expressed as a pH of 4 or a pH of 8. Water has a pH of 7. According to Pirie, the student of molecular biology may have to create a new definition to describe the 'livingness' of a thing, to place accurately in the scale of life a macromolecule, a microorganism, a tree, a planet, an animal, or a man.

The concept of the continuity of life, from the atoms that were formed during the birth of a star to man, is strengthened by our acceptance of Darwinian evolution. We think of the process as having taken place in stages, from inorganic evolution to organic evolution and then to biological evolution. During the genesis of a star, the elements of the periodic table were formed: hydrogen, carbon, nitrogen, oxygen, phosphorus, magnesium, sulphur etc., the atoms that were necessary to give us the small molecules related to living processes – methane, ammonia, water, hydrogen sulphide, phosphate etc. The molecules then underwent further changes to give rise to the amino acids, the carbohydrates, the purines, and pyrimidines. The macromolecules, nucleic acids and proteins, which were then formed interacted with each other, giving rise to the first biota. Subsequent biological evolution accounted for the development of the entire biosphere.

The continuity of life can be traced from the birth of a star (far left), in which first the elements are formed, and then the life-forming molecules such as ammonia, water and methane. These in turn give rise to the amino acids, carbohydrates, purines and pyrimidines, and to the more complex proteins and nucleic acids. Interacting together over aeons of time, these would at last have developed the first primitive beginnings of what can be called life

The 'Sombrero Hat' nebula, seen edge-on, shows a dark band right across the disk. From such a cloud as this, of hydrogen and dust particles, our own solar system must have evolved

The aphorism that we are the stuff of which stars are made is more than rhetoric. The atoms which constitute the different molecules of the atmosphere, the crust of the earth, the lakes, rivers, and ocean waters, plants and animals, were generated during the birth of the galaxies.

Spectroscopic studies have provided us with data on the abundance of elements in the sun and stars.

Almost 95 per cent of living matter is made up of hydrogen, carbon, nitrogen, and oxygen. These are the very elements which are most abundant in the cosmos. A glance at a table of the composition of the sun shows us that, apart from helium, an inert gas which is inactive and cannot combine with anything else, hydrogen, carbon, nitrogen, and oxygen are the most common in our solar system.

Hydrogen occupies a preeminent place. Of every hundred atoms in the universe, ninety-three are hydrogen atoms. By weight, hydrogen makes up seventy-six per cent of all matter. The heaviest elements add up to only a millionth of the weight of the universe.

When our planet was formed from the primordial solar nebula, the cloud of hydrogen which

Composition of the sun

Hydrogen	87·0 per cent
Helium	12·9
Oxygen	0·025
Nitrogen	0·02
Carbon	0·01
Magnesium	0·003
Silicon	0·002
Iron	0·001
Sulphur	0·001
Others	0·038

Composition of stellar material

Hydrogen	81·76 per cent
Helium	18·17
Oxygen	0·03
Magnesium	0·02
Nitrogen	0·01
Silicon	0·006
Sulphur	0·003
Carbon	0·003
Iron	0·001
Others	0·001

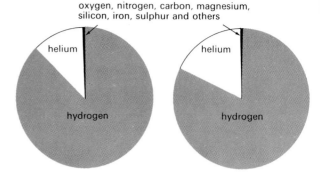

oxygen, nitrogen, carbon, magnesium, silicon, iron, sulphur and others

helium

helium

hydrogen

hydrogen

Ninety-nine point nine per cent of the matter in the universe is hydrogen or helium (the proportion of helium to hydrogen in the Sun is a little less than the universal average). All the other elements, plentiful though they may seem, crowd into the thin wedge that represents the remaining tenth of one per cent

enveloped it, as it revolved with the dust particles in orbit around the central dense mass, played a vital role in determining the kind of molecules present. The study of chemical reactions makes it clear that if there is a large amount of hydrogen, the carbon atoms that are present in the gases and the dust particles will combine with the hydrogen to give rise to methane (CH_4). The equilibrium constant, which is a measure of the tendency, or driving force, of carbon reacting with hydrogen to give methane, is high. So is it with nitrogen. The nitrogen present in the early dust cloud would have combined with the hydrogen to give rise to ammonia (NH_3). The oxygen present would have yielded water. When the planet was being formed, the hydrogen, methane, ammonia, and water gave the primitive atmosphere of the earth a non-oxygenic character.

We have other evidence that suggests that this must have been the case. The larger planets, like Jupiter and Saturn, have held their early atmosphere on account of their very high gravitational forces, which did not allow the escape of many of the gases that were present during the very early stages of planetary formation. Spectroscopic observation of these planets reveals the presence of methane, ammonia, water and hydrogen. If the pristine atmosphere of the earth was similar to the atmospheres of the giant planets, we could conclude that methane, ammonia, and water vapour were indeed present in early times.

Other considerations which lead us to believe that the primordial atmosphere of the earth was reducing (non-oxygenic) in nature stem from the fact that meteorites, which are presumed to be remnants of the solar nebula, contain metals in their reduced form. The chemical effect of the ubiquitous hydrogen is a dominant fact in the universe.

Chinese broad axe, c. 1000 BC, thought to have been made from an iron meteorite. If meteorites are remnants of the solar nebula, the metals they contain, not being oxidized, suggest the absence of oxygen from the primeval atmosphere

The primeval atmosphere

We have reason to believe that the atmosphere which the earth inherited from the primordial solar nebula was lost during its formation. This conclusion is reached from the observation that the noble gases such as helium, neon and argon are more abundant in the cosmos than in our present-day atmosphere. Another atmosphere, secondary in nature and very similar to the first, resulted from emission of gases from the earth's interior.

During the early stages of the earth's formation, volcanic activity was probably rampant throughout its surface. As the embryonic earth began to take shape, the gravitational forces caused contractions in the crust. A great amount of heat must have been generated in this process. The radioactivity which accumulated inside the earth must have also raised the temperature of its core to very high levels. The gases vented from within the earth, devoid of oxygen, were the raw material from which arose the organic compounds leading to large molecules and the first living organism.

How did the transition take place from an atmosphere with essentially no free oxygen into one with about 20 per cent oxygen? The presence of free oxygen is unique in the solar system. How did this oxygen arise? Several factors contributed to this build-up. The water vapour present in our early atmosphere was, to some extent, dissociated by the ultraviolet light which came streaming down from the sun. The water was broken down into hydrogen and oxygen. The oxygen, being a heavier gas, was held by the earth's gravitational force while the hydrogen, being lighter, escaped into space.

Photosynthesis, the process by which green plants convert solar energy for their growth and development, was largely responsible for the

Water vapour (H₂O) in the primeval atmosphere must have been broken into its constituent atoms by ultra-violet radiation from the sun. Hydrogen, being light, leaked out into space; the oxygen atoms combined into ozone (O₃), forming a layer through which little of the radiation could penetrate. Only under this shield could life begin

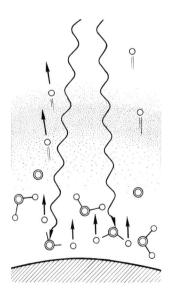

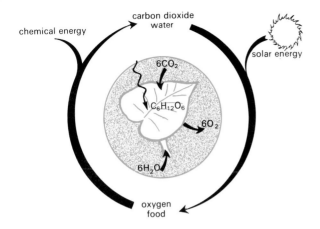

accumulation of oxygen in our atmosphere. The photodissociation of water by ultraviolet light would have reached a certain level beyond which no more water could have been dissociated. When water was decomposed into hydrogen and oxygen, some of the oxygen molecules would, in turn, give rise to ozone (O_3), which acts as a filter for short-wavelength ultraviolet light. The ozone layer which today exists high up in the atmosphere is a protective umbrella from the lethal ultraviolet rays of the sun. When such a layer was formed, the powerful ultraviolet light could not reach the molecules of water any further. On account of this self-regulating mechanism, the amount of oxygen in the atmosphere would not have reached a very high level if the photochemical disintegration of water was the only source of oxygen. But by now, early life must have developed the process of photosynthesis; in this process, light was absorbed, carbon dioxide was converted into various molecules necessary for the living organism, and the oxygen released into the atmosphere began to accumulate.

In the life-giving cycle of photosynthesis, plants use the physical energy of sunlight to convert carbon dioxide and water into the chemical energy of complex compounds such as sugars and fats, giving off oxygen as they do so. Without this process, the animal kingdom could neither eat nor breathe

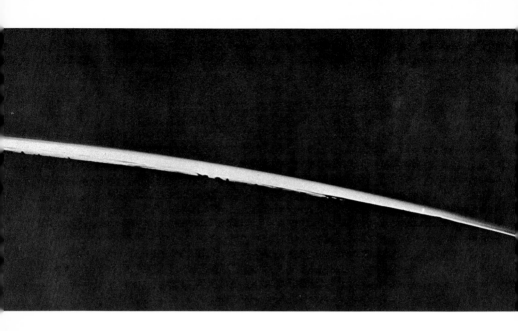

The thin, life-preserving shell of the earth's atmosphere shows up in this photograph taken from an orbiting spacecraft

The coming of oxygen

Early life was a non-oxygenic, anaerobic life. The primitive organisms which arose in the primordial oceans were probably heterotrophs, that is, they had their food synthesized for them. There was plenty of food available in the oceans, and the first microorganisms had only to feast on them. But gradually, with the unfurling of the ozone umbrella, the powerful solar energy required for photochemical synthesis did not reach the lower terrestrial atmosphere close to the oceans. No further organic compounds could be synthesized. A period of starvation was in store, and there must have been a wholesale massacre at this point. Only the more resourceful organisms were able to develop the fine art of photosynthesis to use the light that still filtered through the ozone layer. In so doing, further free oxygen was released into the atmosphere. This is the beginning of the accumulation of oxygen.

Gradually, as land plants were evolved, and trees and plants began to develop on the once barren earth, photosynthesis became the one single method by which light energy from the sun was absorbed, and the production of oxygen became commonplace.

The sequence of events which took place before and after the transition may be represented by a diagram in the shape of an hourglass. The lower part of the hourglass represents the period when the atmosphere was without oxygen, ultraviolet light reached the surface of the primordial oceans, and organic matter was synthesized in great abundance. The build-up of the ozone shield and the resulting disappearance of large numbers of early organisms are represented by the narrowing of the hourglass. Some organisms were able to escape this bottleneck. The burgeoning biosphere, with the accompanying evolution of free oxygen, is depicted by the broad and spreading upper section of the hourglass.

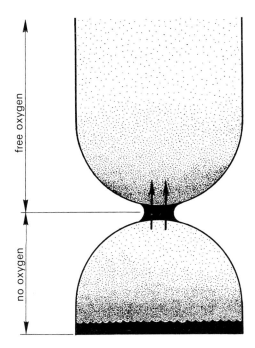

free oxygen

no oxygen

The hourglass shape symbolizes the long, slow transition from the primeval atmosphere, with no oxygen (bottom), to the oxygen-rich atmosphere of today. The narrow neck is the gradual build-up of the ozone shield

It is sometimes erroneously supposed that oxygen is absolutely necessary for life. This is indeed not the case for we know of a large number of organisms which can flourish without oxygen. These anaerobic organisms may be considered fossil organisms, the vestigial traces of the kind of life that existed before free oxygen became an essential factor in our environment.

Geochemists who have studied the crust of the earth have speculated on how long it took for this transition to take place. They believe that there is sufficient evidence to suggest that during this early period of the earth's history the atmosphere must have been non-oxygenic. Some of the most primitive microfossils, dated to as far back as three and a half billion years ago, have also exemplified some structural features characteristic of a photosynthetic apparatus. Some micropaleontologists have described these as algae-like. On the basis of this contention, photosynthesis in a rudimentary form may have existed very early in the history of the earth, and possibly developed in stages into a more efficient process out of sheer necessity.

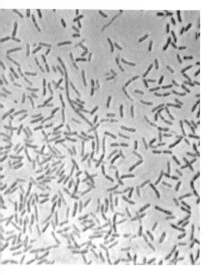

Even now, some living organisms can exist without oxygen, as these bacteria, here shown magnified 1,150 times

Recent observations of the interstellar medium made by radio-astronomers may have a bearing on our concepts of chemical evolution. Interestingly, these experiments have given us some evidence for the very molecules that we have argued should be present in the early atmosphere of any planet, the kind of molecules that must have been formed during the birth of a star. Ammonia and water vapour have been identified by a number of radio-astronomers. As we shall see later, if methane, water and ammonia are present, molecules such as formaldehyde (HCHO), and hydrogen cyanide (HCN) can be formed. Both these molecules have been recently detected in interstellar space. Among other molecules recently reported was cyano-

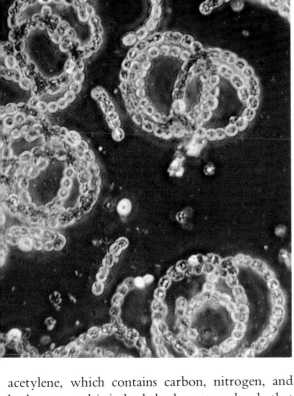

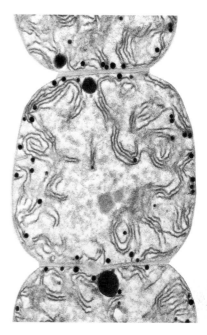

acetylene, which contains carbon, nitrogen, and hydrogen, and is indeed the largest molecule that has been observed, so far, in the interstellar medium. Carbon monoxide, cyanogen, formamide, and acetonitrile appear to be present. These occur in the interstellar medium only in small amount. However, the fact that they are present leads us to believe that they may have been formed from the early mixtures of gases that were the result of the cataclysmic reactions which accompany the birth of stars. Radio-astronomers have provided us with fresh evidence for the true nature of the primordial atmosphere of a planet during the early stages of its evolution.

Photosynthesis of a rudimentary kind, which has probably evolved little since the process first developed, is shown by blue-green algae, primitive single-celled organisms more like bacteria than the plants they actually are. Above left: strings of Nostoc, × 400. Above: an electron micrograph shows, at a magnification of 18,000 times, the twisting double membranes of the simple photosynthetic system

49

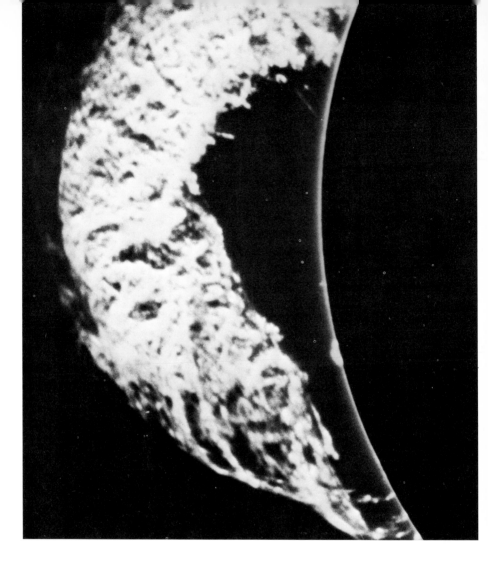

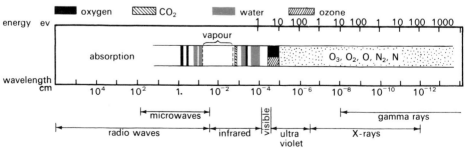

SOURCES OF ENERGY

Solar energy beat down upon the juvenile earth with its atmosphere of methane, ammonia, water and nitrogen. The sun was the most powerful source of energy for the earth. The spectrum of the sun has energy of various wavelengths, from the very shortest to the longest, the shorter-wavelength light being the most energetic. The solar flux about four and a half billion years ago could not have been very different from what it is today. A star like our sun is in the main sequence and, once it reaches this stage in its evolutionary development, it remains stable for several billion years. The energy flux emanating from the sun must thus have been steady over the last five billion years.

A large amount of the energetic ultraviolet rays were available for organic synthesis. The ultraviolet light which acted on the early atmosphere must have dissociated the components of the atmosphere into radicals, ions, and activated atoms. These would have recombined to generate small molecules which, in turn, would have given rise to larger molecules. The longer-wavelength light, although it may not have been powerful enough to break down molecules like methane, ammonia and water, must have been useful for synthesis of

A million-mile arch of incandescent hydrogen (above opposite) symbolizes the ceaseless energy of the sun, probably still the same, to within a few per cent, as it was four and a half billion years ago. Opposite, below: in the spectrum of electromagnetic radiation – continuous from the ultra-short gamma rays to the longest radio waves – different wavelengths are absorbed by different forms of matter. The shorter ultraviolet rays, absorbed by the early atmosphere, would have imparted enough energy to start a chain reaction of ionization, recombination, and synthesis of larger and larger molecules

larger molecules. Organic compounds, such as amino acids or the nucleic acid bases, formed by the action of the energetic ultraviolet light, could absorb light at longer wavelengths so that a chain reaction would have been started. Today, we see that the porphyrin molecule in living organisms is able to absorb the longer-wavelength light. If similar molecules were formed before life began,

then there was a reasonably good chance that much of the long-wavelength ultraviolet light would also have been harnessed for the early stages of pre-biological evolution.

Electrical discharges must have provided another source of energy during the earliest times. Lightning in its many forms, whether forked or sheet, is of frequent occurrence in the atmosphere of today.

Lightning, common enough today, must have been responsible for much organic synthesis in primeval earth conditions

Such electrical displays must have been commonplace under primordial conditions. A flash of lightning through a cloud of methane and ammonia could have generated a great deal of organic matter. While this form of energy may have been less abundant than the energy that was available from the sun, it may have been more effective in generating organic molecules. The ultraviolet light from the sun reached only the upper atmosphere, and organic molecules that were synthesized may not have reached the oceans. These molecules may have been destroyed by solar radiation before they reached the protective reaches of surface waters. On the other hand, electrical discharges would have been close to the earth's surface and organic matter could have been readily transferred to the oceans.

Radioactivity, which is widespread in the earth's crust, is also a very powerful storehouse of energy. The principal radioactive sources of the earth today are radioactive potassium and radioactive uranium – potassium 40, uranium 238, and uranium 235. Potassium 40 appears to be the most predominant. It is also perhaps the most effective since potassium is soluble in water, and the radioactivity may have been dispersed through the oceans. The energy of potassium is in the form of powerful beta and gamma rays. These can penetrate through the water, or through the crust. However, in the case of uranium, most of the energy would be emitted in the form of alpha particles, which are not particularly powerful or penetrating. According to calculations based on the abundance of potassium today, and tracing back from the half-life of radioactive potassium, we can calculate that, about two and a half billion years ago, the radioactive energy present on the earth would have been of the order of 12×10^{19} calories. Although

this is only about one-thirtieth of the amount of energy available in the short-wavelength region of the ultraviolet spectrum, it may have been important on account of its proximity to the earth's surface.

Heat energy must also have played a role on the primitive earth. Volcanic activity must have been prevalent during most of the earth's formative period. The gases emanating from a volcano could pass over molten lava and reach the oceans, giving rise to vast amounts of organic matter. Apart from

Glowing streams of lava criss-cross the slopes of Hawaii's Kilauea volcano; the fierce volcanic heat, and the gases passing over the molten lava and flowing down to the oceans, would have been a rich source of organic synthesis

The newly emerged island of Surt-sey, off the south coast of Iceland

57

Icelandic hot springs at Namaskard: there must have been a vast amount of heat energy available when the earth was young

volcanic activity, the present-day abundance of hot springs testifies to their availability as a source of energy when the world was young.

Solar heat must also be taken into account. Once molecules were synthesized by ultraviolet light or electrical discharges or by the action of ionizing radiations and accumulated along the shores of the primordial oceans, heat from the sun could have been a factor in further synthesis. It is conceivable that some of the lagoons along the oceans could have evaporated, and the organic matter in them could then have been exposed to direct heat from the sun.

It has also been suggested that the shock waves generated by meteorites passing through the primitive atmosphere may have given rise to a large amount of organic matter. As a meteorite passes through an atmosphere, intensely high temperatures and pressures are momentarily generated. Some of these temperatures may be as high as 20,000° C., with pressures of the order of 15,000 to 20,000 atmospheres. A dissociation of the molecules may have taken place on a large scale. The quenching which follows immediately would have condensed these dissociated molecules, and recombination would have occurred fairly rapidly.

Recent calculations by Adolf Hochstim of Wayne State University, based on meteorites that pass through the earth's present atmosphere, have shown that a meteorite with a diameter of about 11 kilometres entering the earth's atmosphere at a speed of about 11 kilometres per second, may

Meteors, setting up shock waves in the atmosphere, would have generated energy for dissociation and recombination of molecules. This Victorian print shows a meteor that passed over the fields and hedgerows of London's Fulham Road in 1850

generate as much as 10^{12} (one million million) tons of organic matter in its wake. In an atmosphere without oxygen, and if methane, ammonia and water were available, it is possible that the amount of organic matter synthesized may have been very much more.

In the collapse of a bubble, a shock wave can be generated. This is a phenomenon which may have taken place on the surface of the oceans. During the action of the waves, a large number of bubbles may have been formed which collapsed and, in so doing, released energy for synthesis. Thunder may also be responsible for organic synthesis. Sonic

booms are known to release large amounts of energy.

It is obvious that a variety of energy sources must have been available for the formation of organic compounds upon the primitive earth. Some of these may have been useful for particular aspects of this synthesis. The variety and intensity of the action may have given rise to different products. In the laboratory, most of these forms of energy have been used in order to simulate the conditions on the primitive earth. These experiments have provided many results which substantiate the hypothesis of chemical evolution.

A meteor of a size to make the famous Meteor Crater in Arizona could generate, in its wake, organic matter to the tune of millions of tons

Right: Dr Stanley L. Miller, and the apparatus he used to synthesize amino acids with an electric discharge. Below: diagram of the Miller experiment. Steam circulates from the boiling water at lower left, through the 'atmosphere' of ammonia, methane and hydrogen, and down past the condenser. After a week of sparking, the water at the bottom was found to be rich in organic compounds

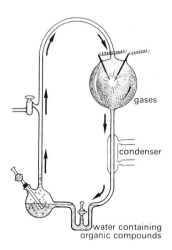

gases

condenser

water containing
organic compounds

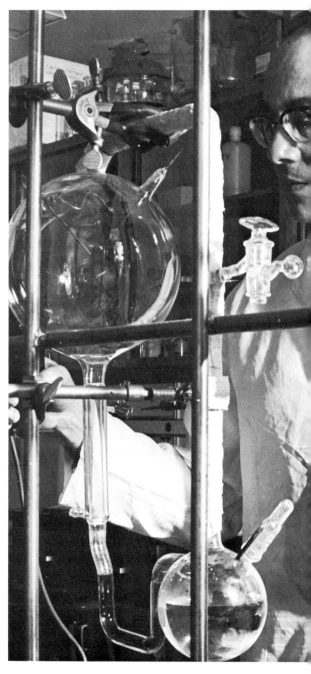

LABORATORY EXPERIMENTS 5

In the simulation of primitive earth conditions in the laboratory, electrical discharges have been used most widely. Historically, the reason for the extensive use of this form of energy may be related to the ease with which the equipment could be set up. In the early part of this century, Heber's attempts at organic synthesis with electric discharges led him to assert that the atoms that result from the passing of a spark through a primitive atmosphere can recombine to give practically any molecule under the sun.

One of the classic experiments in the field was done in 1953 by Stanley Miller, working with Harold Urey at the University of Chicago. The apparatus that Miller built was designed to circulate methane, ammonia, hydrogen and water, components of the earth's primitive atmosphere, past an electric spark. Electrodes were placed in a 5-litre flask, and a small tesla coil produced the spark. Boiling water produced steam which helped to circulate the gases through the system. After a week of sparking, the water containing organic compounds was analyzed. The results were beyond belief. A number of substances related to life were synthesized. Among them were four of the amino

Among the substances Miller found in his apparatus were four common amino acids – glycine, alanine, aspartic acid and glutamic acid. Crystals of glycine, magnified 120 times in polarized light, are seen above

acids commonly found in protein: glycine, alanine, aspartic acid and glutamic acid. In this mixture were some of the simplest of the fatty acids, formic, acetic and propionic. Urea, a compound which has an important role in many biological processes, was also identified.

These experiments were repeated by a number of investigators, Abelson in the U.S., Pavlovskaia and Pasynskii in the USSR, and Heyns, Walter, and Meyer in Germany. At the Carnegie Institute in Washington, Abelson used a variety of mixtures of gases. As long as the composition of the gases was reducing in nature, organic molecules were produced. When oxidizing conditions were em-

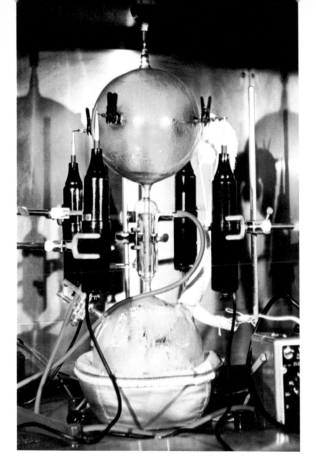

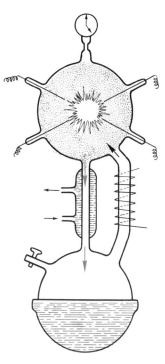

ployed, no amino acids resulted. Indirectly, these results implied that the early atmosphere of the earth had to be non-oxygenic if organic molecules necessary for life had to be formed.

The action of lightning in the primitive atmosphere has been simulated in a number of experiments. In the author's laboratory, the apparatus used for experiments of this type consists of a dumbbell-shaped flask, the upper flask representing the atmosphere, the lower flask, which contains the water, representing the primordial seas. Methane and ammonia are contained in the flask. A condenser connects the two globes. A side arm, which is kept hot, enables the moisture to reach the upper

A similar apparatus in the author's laboratory simulates the action of lightning in an atmosphere of methane, water vapour (from the lower flask) and ammonia. After 24 hours of lightning 'flashes', there is a dark-brown deposit of hydrocarbons on the sides of the upper flask and other compounds in solution

flask, condense, and fall back into the ocean below. Electrodes through the upper regions provide for the passage of the electric discharge simulating lightning. The lower flask is generally maintained at about 100° C. in order to enable the water to vaporize and reach the upper levels where the discharge takes place. In the spark itself, the temperatures may go up to about 5,000° C. to 10,000° C. However, the rest of the flask is at a much lower temperature. Organic matter thus accumulates in the 'ocean' below.

In a typical experiment, tesla coils, which are used in laboratories for the detection of leaks, provide a useful source of high voltage for the sparking system. In a ten-litre flask, methane and ammonia are introduced up to a pressure of about one atmosphere. About one hundred millilitres of water are contained in the flask below. At the end of a 24-hour experiment, large deposits of organic compounds are found in the flask. There is a dark brown deposit which contains hydrocarbons and some nitrogenous material. About 45 per cent of the initial carbon appears in the lower flask in the form of dissolved organic matter. Haldane's description of a 'primordial soup' was indeed prophetic.

In simulating the use of ionizing radiation, in 1963 Ponnamperuma and Calvin used the electron beam of a linear accelerator at Berkeley as a convenient source of electrons, replacing the beta particles from radioactive potassium. The atmosphere is now contained in a long horizontal tube. The beta particles are shot in through the end window, and interact with the mixture of methane, ammonia, and water vapour contained in the tube. A cold finger suspended above the little flask, which now serves as our primordial ocean, enables any organic compound synthesized to fall back into

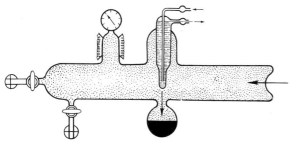

the ocean. The organic compounds which accumulate are analyzed for the presence of life-related molecules.

We have seen earlier, in our discussion of the different kinds of energy which are available for synthesis under primordial conditions, that ultraviolet light was a very important source of energy. Although many experiments have been designed for the use of ultraviolet light, not many have been successful because of many inherent experimental difficulties. Methane, ammonia, and water dissociate well below 2,000 Angstrom units. To utilize the short-wavelength light for photochemical synthesis, the reaction vessels need to be fitted with special windows. Lithium fluoride, for example, is one of the few materials that will transmit light in this region of the spectrum.

In 1957, Groth and Weysenhoff in Germany, and Terenin in the Soviet Union, were able to synthesize glycine and alanine by the use of ultraviolet light.

Powerful light sources in which helium and argon are the ionized gases have become available since then. One particular lamp that has been employed at the Ames Research Center is a 15-atmosphere argon source. The total energy in the spectrum between 1,000 and 2,000 Angstrom units has been calculated as being equivalent to about 10^{19} photons per square centimetre per year. This amount of energy is almost four orders of magnitude greater than the solar energy in that region. With such equipment, a laboratory experiment can be designed to achieve in a brief period what may have taken long years under natural conditions.

Several experiments have been performed to show the effects of heat in organic synthesis. The work of Sidney Fox of the University of Miami has centred around the thermal model of biochemical origins. In a typical simulation experiment, the mixture of gases was passed through a hot tube maintained at about 1,000° C. The heated surface of the tube would represent the hot lava over which the gases emanating from a primordial volcano may have passed before reaching the ocean. Nitriles, the precursors of amino acids, are

To simulate in the laboratory the ultraviolet radiation that poured down from the sun on to the primeval earth is more difficult. In the author's laboratory, however, argon gas at 15 atmospheres' pressure has been used as a source (opposite), and organic compounds have been successfully synthesized

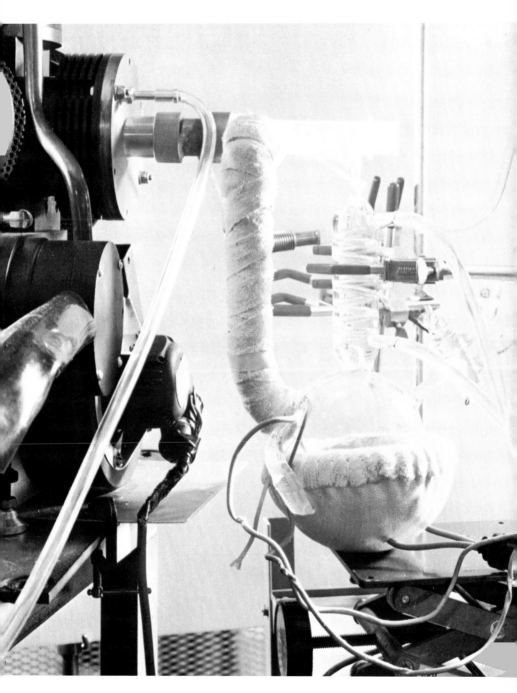

produced by the heat. These compounds react with water to give amino acids. The methane and ammonia break down at these temperatures and recombine to produce a mixture of compounds containing amino acids and hydrocarbons.

Laboratory attempts to reproduce the action of hypersonic energy, as in the shock wave created by a meteorite passing through the atmosphere (p. 59), have been confined to a few instances. In one example, a metal ball was projected at high velocity into a tube containing methane, ammonia, and water, to simulate a meteorite passing through the atmosphere. In other instances, shock tubes have been used. The high temperatures generated in the shock tubes give rise to the intermediates in the synthesis of larger molecules.

All these different types of experimentation and simulation of prebiological conditions have produced many of the building blocks of life, such as amino acids, purines, pyrimidines, carbohydrates, hydrocarbons etc. The first problem that confronts the chemist is the identification of these compounds in the primordial soup re-created in the laboratory. He must then establish a scientifically acceptable rationale for the formation of the molecules necessary for life.

A Lichtenberg figure (opposite) is a laboratory visualization of the complex ionization patterns produced in air by an electric discharge at voltages comparable to those of a lightning strike

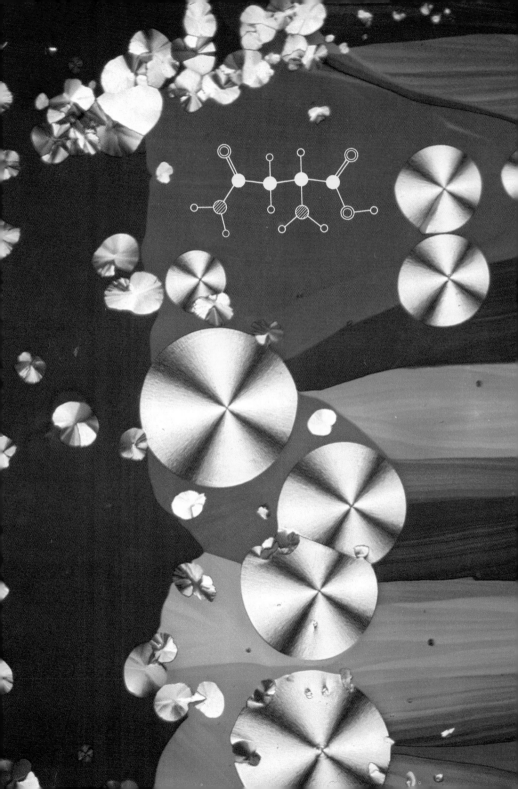

SYNTHESIS OF SMALL MOLECULES 6

Laboratory investigations on the origin of life have been primarily focused on the origin of amino acids. These are the building blocks of proteins. In structure, they are positively charged at one end of the molecule and negatively at the other, giving them, unusually, the characteristics of both an acid and a base. Peptides, which are combinations of amino acids, appear when an amino (or positively charged) group of one molecule dovetails into the carboxyl (or negatively charged) group of another. This process of building up might continue till more and more single units come together and result in protein chains.

One reason why the amino acids were first studied in detail is because they were the most important molecules in life and could be detected easily. In Miller's 1953 experiment, several amino acids were observed. Of these, glycine, alanine, aspartic acid and glutamic acid are among those commonly found in protein. There were also some amino acids which are not generally identified when proteins of plants or animals are broken down into their constituents. The unusual acids identified were sarcosine, β-alanine, and α-amino-butyric acid. The presence of the 'non-protein'

Opposite: crystals of the amino acid asparagine, magnified in polarized light. The amino group at one end (H_2N) is positively charged, the carboxyl group (COOH) at the other is negative; the molecule as a whole is neutral, but joins readily with others

Overleaf: the amino acid family. Note the group that is common to and characteristic of all amino acids – basic at one end (H_2N, the amino group) and acidic at the other (COOH): some twenty variations on a theme

MONO AMINO MONO CARBOXYLIC	$H_2N - CH_2 - COOH$ glycine	$\begin{array}{c} CH_3 \\ | \\ H_2N - CH - COOH \end{array}$ alanine
HYDROXY		$\begin{array}{c} CH_2OH \\ | \\ H_2N - CH - COOH \end{array}$ serine
MONO AMINO DICARBOXYLIC		$\begin{array}{c} COOH \\ | \\ CH_2 \\ | \\ H_2N - CH - COOH \end{array}$ aspartic
BASIC	$\begin{array}{c} CH_2 - NH_2 \\ | \\ CH_2 \\ | \\ CH_2 \\ | \\ CH_2 \\ | \\ H_2N - CH - COOH \end{array}$ lysine	
SULPHUR-CONTAINING	$\begin{array}{c} CH_2SH \\ | \\ H_2N - CH - COOH \end{array}$ cysteine	
AROMATIC	$\begin{array}{c} CH_2 \\ | \\ H_2N - CH - COOH \end{array}$ phenylalanine	$\begin{array}{c} OH \\ CH_2 \\ | \\ H_2N - CH - COOH \end{array}$ tyrosine
HETEROCYCLIC	$\begin{array}{c} COOH \\ | \\ C - CH_2 - CH \\ \quad\quad\quad\quad | \\ CH \quad\quad\quad NH_2 \\ N \\ H \end{array}$ tryptophan	

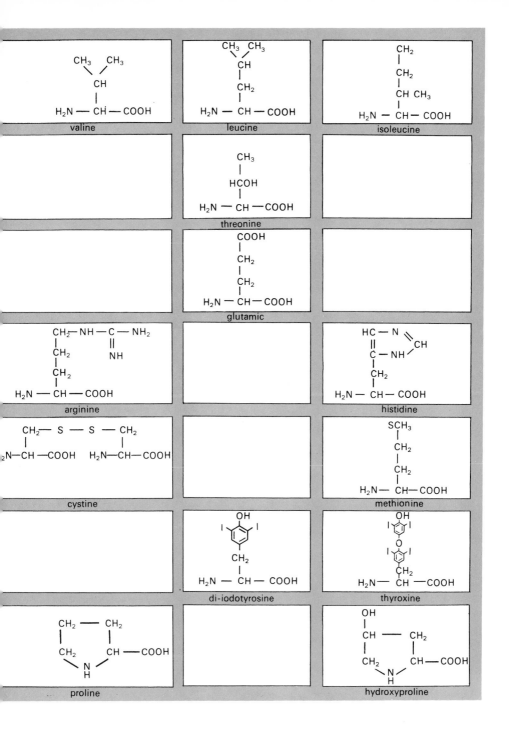

amino acids in the products of these experiments leads us to believe that only a small number of amino acids were selected for incorporation into the living organism.

The understanding of the intricate chemical pathways by which amino acids may have been formed under pre-life conditions is an essential requirement in the study of chemical evolution. We learn that these molecules were formed according to the common rules which govern the interaction of atoms, radicals and molecules. The reaction schemes are simple and straightforward, reminiscent of those which we have learned in our study of basic organic chemistry.

The mechanism for the synthesis of the amino acids identified in the primordial soup has been carefully studied. There were two possibilities for the formation of these compounds. According to classical organic theory, amino acids are generally synthesized from aldehydes and nitriles. Formaldehyde (HCHO) is the simplest member of the aldehyde series, while hydrogen cyanide (HCN) may be considered to be the parent nitrile. As long ago as 1881, the German chemist Strecker had suggested the mode of synthesis that bears his name.

Possible pathways of chemical evolution: molecules synthesized by radiation energy interact in the 'primordial soup' to produce nucleic acid bases, perhaps even the sugars. In shallow lagoons, on a clay bottom, alternately wet and baking dry, the earliest big molecules could have formed

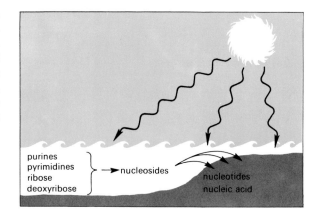

purines
pyrimidines
ribose
deoxyribose
} ⟶ nucleosides

nucleotides
nucleic acid

In the first step, an aldehyde and a nitrile combine in the presence of ammonia to give an intermediate product:

$$RCHO + NH_3 + HCN \rightleftarrows RCH(NH_2)CN + H_2O$$

On treatment with water, this results in an amino acid:

$$RCH(NH_2)CN + 2H_2O$$
$$\rightarrow RCH(NH_2)COOH + NH_3$$

It is possible that the aldehydes and the nitriles were formed in the gas phase of the spark, in the upper atmosphere of the dumbbell-shaped system. The two would combine together to form the precursor -amino nitrile

$$RCHO + HCN \rightleftarrows RCH(OH)CN$$

which, on reaching the water, would have produced the amino acids:

$$RCH(OH)CN + 2H_2O$$
$$\rightarrow RCH(OH)COOH + NH_3$$

An alternative hypothesis would be that the amino acids themselves were directly synthesized in the gas phase. Subsequent research has shown that it was very likely that their formation took place by way of the Strecker synthesis. The examination of the reaction products indicated the presence of aldehydes and cyanides, and the rate of formation of amino acids was proportional to the disappearance of the aldehydes and the nitriles. This was observed in an independent experiment in which a nitrile and an aldehyde were refluxed together.

Amino acids have also been synthesized by simulating the energy of the sun. Not only have primitive mixtures been exposed to ultraviolet light, but also some compounds which we can reasonably expect to be formed from primitive atmospheres, such as ammonium formate and hydrogen cyanide, have been used as raw materials for these investigations. In each case, amino acids have been identified. Ionizing radiation and heat have also been employed as sources of energy in related studies.

The formation of amino acids under simulated prebiotic conditions suggests that they were readily formed on the primitive earth. These results cannot, however, be construed to mean that the question of the origin of amino acids is solved and perhaps does not deserve any more attention.

Several aspects of this problem need further study. Many of the amino acids formed by the action of electrical discharges, ultraviolet light, heat, or shock waves do not occur naturally in biological material. Why were only twenty amino acids incorporated in natural proteins? In addition, further experimentation is required to establish the synthesis of some of the naturally occurring amino acids which have not yet been prepared otherwise than from organic material.

The nucleic acids

An objective of paramount importance in prebiotic chemistry is to understand how nucleic acids, which are at the very core of genetic organization, appeared before life. A glimpse into the manner in which the single units of the DNA and RNA molecule came about will be a first step towards this goal.

In DNA (p.34) there are four bases, adenine, guanine, cytosine, and thymine. In RNA, uracil replaces thymine. Many attempts have been made to demonstrate the possible prebiotic origin of these molecules. In one of the earliest efforts to establish the formation of a purine under primordial conditions, Juan Oro, working at the University of

Houston, obtained adenine by the action of heat on ammonium cyanide. A close look at the molecule of adenine shows us the empirical formula $H_5C_5N_5$ which may be considered to be five molecules of hydrogen cyanide joined together. The synthesis of hydrogen cyanide would thus lead logically to the appearance of adenine.

Hydrogen cyanide, although a deadly poison in today's biosphere, probably occurred in abundance on the primitive earth and was essential to prebiotic processes. Spectroscopic data show that this compound is also present in the comets. When a comet moves towards the sun, the cyanide band is the single most predominant line in the spectrum. This is of interest since the solar nebula from which our planets arose is considered to have been similar in

adenine   guanine

From hydrogen cyanide, abundant in the early, pre-oxygen atmosphere, two of the nucleic acid bases, adenine and guanine, could have originated. Hydrogen cyanide is one atom each of hydrogen, carbon and nitrogen: each of these bases has five atoms of each, guanine an oxygen atom in addition. The diagram above shows, in chemical terms, the pathways by which adenine and guanine could have arisen

The Ikeya-Seki comet of 1965, photographed over Canberra (left). Hydrogen cyanide, abundant on the primeval earth, is prominent among the gases that make up a comet's tail

79

composition to comets. Recent radioastronomical data have also revealed its presence in the interstellar medium. Laboratory investigations have shown that hydrogen cyanide is formed in copious yields from methane, ammonia and water. The electrical discharge experiments alone give rise to about 15 per cent of hydrogen cyanide.

O ORIGIN   BUTANOL—FORMIC ACID—WATER

PROPANOL—AMMONIA—WATER

ADENINE

The 'fingerprints' of adenine in a paper chromatogram proved the success of the electron bombardment experiment (p. 66). The mixture of molecules generated was separated out by a flow of solvents; by the use of radioactive carbon in the methane (CH₄) of the simulated atmosphere, every carbon compound shows up as a dark spot on an X-ray film placed over the filter paper

Adenine was also identified by Ponnamperuma and his co-workers among the molecules formed by the action of ionizing radiation on primitive atmospheres. When a mixture of methane, ammonia and water was exposed to beta particles from a linear accelerator, adenine was synthesized. Not only was it the single largest non-volatile product that was formed, but the production of adenine was enhanced by the absence of hydrogen. This is not surprising since the carbon in the methane had to be oxidized to appear in the purines. If an excess of hydrogen was there, this process would be hindered since many of the radicals produced would be reconverted to the starting methane. In any event, the high concentration of organic matter on the prebiotic earth probably arose when most of the hydrogen had escaped from this atmosphere.

Although many efforts have been made, the other purines have not been identified in the end-products of experiments with primordial atmospheres. Similar efforts to locate pyrimidines have been very unrewarding.

In order to circumvent this difficulty, many experimenters have attempted to reconstruct cytosine, thymine, and uracil from molecules which may be regarded as second-generation precursors. Some of the end-products of the primitive atmosphere experiments would themselves be the stepping stones to further synthesis. Noteworthy is the work of Leslie Orgel at the Salk Institute. He regarded cyanoacetylene, which is formed when methane and nitrogen are exposed to an electric discharge, as a possible precursor of the pyrimidines. When cyanoacetylene and urea are heated together, cytosine is produced. Urea occurs as a predominant product in most experiments involving methane, ammonia and water. The combination of cyanoacetylene and urea may provide a reasonable pathway for pyrimidine synthesis.

The sugars, ribose and deoxyribose, are integral parts of the nucleic acid molecule. The bases adenine, guanine, cytosine, thymine and uracil are combined together with the sugars to give rise to nucleosides. These, in turn, can combine with phosphate to give nucleotides, the single units of the nucleic acid molecule. Although the primordial soup generated from methane, ammonia, and water has been carefully analyzed for the presence of the sugar component of nucleic acids, no evidence is yet forthcoming for their presence. However, formaldehyde, which we have already described as an intermediate in the synthesis of amino acids, has been detected. It is the simplest of the sugars, and may be considered to be responsible for the origin of the higher members of the series. The recent discovery of formaldehyde in the interstellar

One of the most complex molecules to be discovered in interstellar space is formaldehyde (CH_2O). Using the 140-ft deep-space radio-telescope at Greenbank, West Virginia (below), scientists have picked up its characteristic line (right) from several different sources. Its presence almost certainly guarantees the existence in galactic dust clouds of methane (CH_4), an essential ingredient of the 'primordial broth'

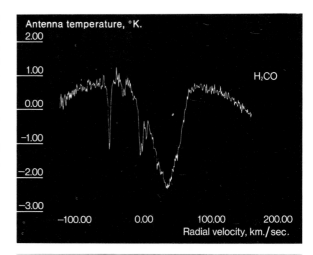

medium has further highlighted the significance of formaldehyde as a primordial molecule.

As early as 1861, Butlerov demonstrated that formaldehyde could be converted to a mixture of sugars when heated in a strong alkaline solution. The primary condensation product of two molecules of formaldehyde is another member of the aldehyde series – glycolaldehyde. This, together with a third molecule of formaldehyde, can give us another precursor of sugars called dihydroxy-acetone. When these two molecules are formed, the pathway towards the sugars of importance to life becomes patent. For those who can read chemical formulae, the process is:

$$2CH_2O \rightarrow CH_2OH \cdot CHO$$
$$CH_2OH \cdot CHO + CH_2O$$
$$\rightarrow CH_2OH \cdot CO \cdot CH_2OH$$
$$CH_2OH \cdot CHO + CH_2OH \cdot CO \cdot CH_2OH$$
$$\rightarrow CH_2OH \cdot CHOH \cdot CHOH \cdot CO \cdot CH_2OH$$

or

$$2CH_2OH \cdot CHO$$
$$\rightarrow CH_2OH \cdot CHOH \cdot CHOH \cdot CHO$$
$$or\ CH_2OH \cdot CO \cdot CHOH \cdot CH_2OH$$
$$2C_4 - [C_8]? \rightarrow C_3 + C_5$$

An intriguing model for the primordial origin of sugars was proposed by Ponnamperuma and Gabel: a hydrothermal spring. Very dilute solutions of formaldehyde were refluxed over clay surfaces such as kaolinite and illite. A mineral such as kaolinite may be considered to reproduce faithfully some of the prebiological conditions which could have existed around a hot spring. Simple refluxing or boiling of the formaldehyde led to condensation reactions and the higher sugars. The five-membered and six-membered sugars (pentoses and hexoses) were most readily obtained in this process.

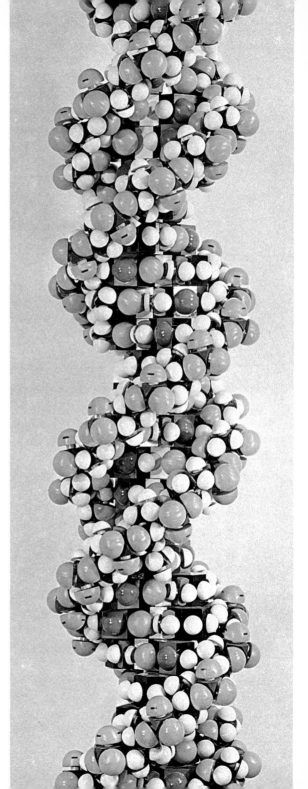

DNA – short for deoxyribo-nucleic acid – is the basic polymer of all living things. This model of the famous 'double helix' places every atom in each nucleotide in a few twists of the long molecule

POLYMERS 7

So far, we have seen that the single units which constitute the nucleic acids and proteins could have been synthesized by the action of the various forms of energy in primitive atmospheres. These small molecules may have been formed directly from the primordial atmosphere, or may have resulted in a stepwise manner from reactive intermediates. The chemist has tried to untangle the process by which the building blocks of life appeared. Although we have not yet solved all the problems, and although we do not still know the detailed scheme for the constituents we have identified, the general pattern of the formation of these compounds appears to be well established. The next stage of experimentation concerns the condensation, or polymerization, of these molecules to give the larger units leading to the nucleic acids and the proteins.

The protein molecule is made up of a string of amino acids. The individual amino acids are linked together by a peptide bond. When two amino acids are brought together, or condensed together, dehydration, or the removal of a molecule of water, takes place. The elimination of a single molecule of water is thus a necessary step in the linking of two amino acids to give a dipeptide. Two dipeptides can combine to give a tetrapeptide, and the process of chain-building can be continued.

Similarly, a nucleic acid molecule consists of a series of nucleotides which are like beads in the chain. Each nucleotide, in turn, is made up of a base, a sugar, and a phosphate. Here again, the mechanism of combination is a condensation and dehydration. A molecule of water has to be removed in order to bring a base and a sugar together to give a nucleoside. When a nucleoside is formed, a phosphate can be added to the nucleoside to give rise to a nucleotide. Two nucleotides combine together to give a dinucleotide. In each case, then, the removal of a molecule of water at every step becomes the mechanism by which the larger molecules are built.

If this process were to take place in an aqueous

The protein molecule is a string of amino acids (right), the 'backbone' consisting of repeating triplets like links in a chain, with different side-groups for each different amino acid (for a key to the element symbols, see p. 34). When two amino acids join up (below), they come together, amino end to carboxyl end, and give up a molecule of water between them (below right). This is the peptide bond

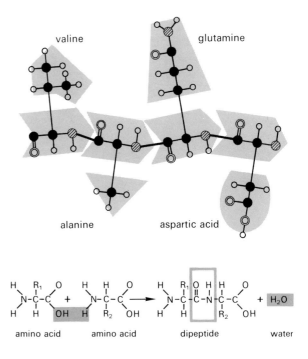

valine

glutamine

alanine

aspartic acid

amino acid   amino acid   dipeptide   water

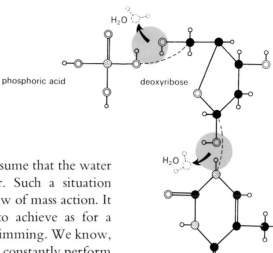

medium, one would have to assume that the water was being removed in water. Such a situation appears to be contrary to the law of mass action. It is as impossible a condition to achieve as for a swimmer to keep dry while swimming. We know, however, that living organisms constantly perform condensation reactions in building biopolymers. This is done by way of the enzymes, which are catalysts helping the molecules over the energy barrier encountered in the seemingly impossible reaction. If such reactions took place in the ocean, it would appear to be a reasonable method for the origin of prebiological macromolecules.

In the formation of nucleic acid a similar process takes place, phosphate linking to sugar and sugar to base with the condensing out of a water molecule

If the removal of water is necessary for the synthesis of a polymer, perhaps a ready method of synthesis would involve the removal of that molecule of water by thermal methods. The heating of the two amino acids together to drive the molecule of water away might have been a simple mechanism. This could also have occurred in the case of the nucleic acid constituents – a base and a sugar could be heated together and a dehydration brought about. Similarly, a nucleoside and a phosphate could be thermally condensed to a nucleotide.

Such a sequence of events would have been feasible on the primordial earth. Bernal was the first to point out that lagoons, when dried up, would have been an ideal locale for the origin of large molecules. Organic material, adsorbed on the clay at the bottom of the lagoons, would have been exposed to solar radiation, and dehydrations would have taken place. The material thus polymerized would have been removed into the oceans by the action of the water. Reactions of this type may also have occurred along the ocean shoreline. The organic matter brought onto the sands would have been adsorbed by the surface of the silicates. Solar radiation would have caused further dehydration. Such a process may be observed to occur even in the present-day oceans. The lagoons that are strung along the waterfronts are occasionally found to be dry. At other times, at high tide for example, the water rushes in and fills these areas. This alternate drying and flooding would have been a very useful method for synthesis of polymers and their removal into the prebiotic ocean.

In innumerable experiments, both these types of reactions have been simulated. Attempts have been made to synthesize polymers in aqueous conditions. Other efforts relate to the simulation of prebiotic dried-up oceans. Dehydration-condensations have been demonstrated in both instances.

Several experimental results illustrate the polymerization which may have taken place in aqueous solutions. For example, the synthesis of peptides has been accomplished, by Calvin at Berkeley and Ponnamperuma at the Ames Research Center, using dilute solutions of amino acids. However, a condensing agent has been necessary in these cases. These condensing agents would substitute for the catalysts, or enzymes, which are responsible for such reactions in biological systems. Here, the pre-biological chemist has taken a leaf from the book of the organic chemists, who have a repertory of reagents which can polymerize amino acids or nucleotides. One of the most celebrated experiments of this type is the synthesis of polynucleotides

by Khorana, using the dicyclohexylcarbodiimides. These carbodiimides are a family of compounds which are substituted cyanides. Among the simplest of these are cyanamid and dicyanamid, which may be considered to be parent compounds of the carbodiimides. Both cyanamid and dicyanamid have been reported to have been formed from the primitive atmosphere when it was exposed to a form of radiation. As catalysts, they may be considered to be truly prebiotic in character.

Shallow lagoons have been suggested as probable sites, with their frequent drying out and flooding, for synthesis of polymers from the prebiotic soup. The teeming plant life of this North Australian lagoon would not, of course, have been part of the scene

In a simple laboratory experiment at Ames, a very dilute solution of two amino acids, glycine and leucine, was exposed to ultraviolet light in the presence of cyanamid. Radioactively labelled acids were used. (The biochemist finds this a useful method of locating the end-products of his reactions: he separates the different products by paper chromatography, and an X-ray film, placed over the paper chromatogram, is darkened by any radioactive compounds present. These dark spots can thus serve as an indication of the presence of different organic compounds.) The peptides diglycine, triglycine, glycylleucine, and leucylglycine were synthesized. The formation of dipeptides under such conditions thus appears to be firmly established. Similar attempts have been made to synthesize nucleotides in aqueous solutions. Although the measure of success has not been as significant as in the case of the dipeptides, some promising results have been observed.

We noted earlier (p. 79) that in the course of experiments with primitive atmospheres, hydrogen

The formation of the peptide bond – and thus the building up of proteins from amino acids – in prebiotic conditions has been demonstrated in the laboratory. Two common amino acids, with ultraviolet light as the energy source, unite in a dipeptide, losing OH from one side and H from the other to form a molecule of water

glycine + leucine → glycyl – leucine

cyanide appears to be a molecule that is almost ubiquitous. In some cases, it was observed that the amino acids that were formed in these experiments appeared in the analysis only after hydrolysis, suggesting that some kind of polymerization may have already taken place in the primordial broth. The reagent which was responsible for such a synthesis could possibly have been the tetramer of hydrogen cyanide. This reaction was therefore carefully examined, and it was demonstrated that if two amino acids are heated together in the presence of the tetramer of hydrogen cyanide, a dipeptide can be formed. Hydrogen cyanide in this instance not only contributes its share to the formation of the purines and the amino acids, but is itself a condensing agent.

The synthesis of polypeptides has received more attention than the synthesis of other biological polymers. This is probably due to the great emphasis that has been placed on the prebiotic origin of proteins. Among the reactions that have been studied are those in which water is absent. In a typical experiment conducted by Fox, a mixture of amino acids, with a large abundance of glutamic and aspartic acid, was heated in a current of nitrogen. Large polymers are formed when the heating takes place at about $180°$ C. to $200°$ C. A melting of the glutamic acid takes place first, and the molten acid acts as a solvent for the other amino acids. This type of condensation has yielded polymers of very large molecular weight.

There is also a suggestion that the backbone of the protein molecule may have been formed as a polynitrile from methane/ammonia experiments. On hydrolysis, these polynitriles would have given rise to the different polypeptides. This interesting idea stems from the fact that in the electrical discharge experiments, or in those involving hydrogen cyanide, a polymer results, with repeating units very much like those of a polypeptide.

Very early in the course of chemical evolution studies, the Japanese scientist Akabori had worked on this postulate. He proposed the hypothesis that, before the proteins as we know them appeared in the prebiotic soup, there was what might be described as the 'fore-protein'. A nitrile randomly synthesized would be adsorbed by a clay surface, and condensations would result because of the catalytic activity of the clay. Subsequent treatment with water under mildly alkaline conditions would hydrolyze the side groups to give rise to the carboxyl groups that are normally present in the protein molecule.

It may be superfluous to recapitulate the vast array of prebiotic condensation agents used for organic synthesis. It is conceivable that there were many methods by which the polypeptides arose. Polyphosphates, apatite, clay minerals, and activated amino acids may have contributed to the synthesis of polymers before life began on the earth. Laboratory experiments clearly demonstrate that a protein molecule could have been formed in the absence of life.

The dehydration/condensation process has given rise to very large molecules. The larger the molecules get, the less they appear to possess the orderly arrangements that are found in contemporary protein molecules. The dogma of molecular biology holds supreme in the field of science related to life processes. The genetic model of the first living organism is therefore of paramount importance. The synthesis of a polynucleotide under simulated primitive earth conditions would be a considerable step forward in the understanding of the origin of life. The DNA molecule is the centre of the universe of reactions responsible for the evolu-

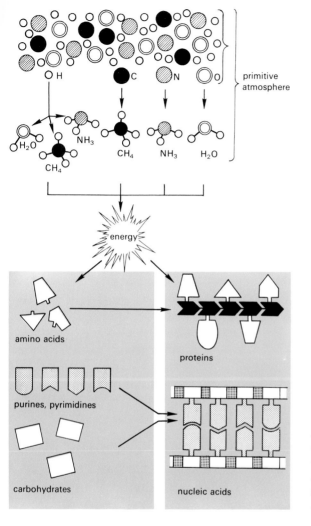

amino acids

proteins

purines, pyrimidines

carbohydrates

nucleic acids

In the primitive atmosphere, the 'life elements' carbon, hydrogen, oxygen and nitrogen were present as water vapour (H_2O), methane (CH_4) and ammonia (NH_3). Powered by various forms of energy they dissociate, re-unite, form amino acids, purines, pyrimidines and carbohydrates. With these ingredients present in the prebiotic soup, proteins could have formed from the amino acids, as experiments have shown. But polymerization of nucleic acids in pre-life conditions has not yet been shown

tion and maintenance of life. Biochemists have recently shown that some of the components of the living cell could be isolated and the reactions necessary for DNA synthesis could be conducted *in vitro*. An enzyme from a cell, together with a small polynucleotide, can be supplied with triphosphates. If the triphosphates are available in abundance, the polynucleotides appear to grow. Such experiments have made it seem more likely that the first nucleic acid could have arisen abiogenically. It is reasonable to suppose that the first polynucleotide may not have been similar to the contemporary polymers. It may have consisted of only a few units.

Several attempts have been made to synthesize nucleic acids by nonenzymic means. High-energy phosphates have been considered to be a necessary requirement for such a step. Polynucleotides have been made at moderate temperatures by the use of phosphates. The experiments done with uridine, in which this nucleoside was heated together with other phosphates giving rise to chains of two, three, and perhaps four nucleotides, open the door to further promising investigations. Some of these reactions have been conducted at temperatures around 150° C. to 160° C. But, even at a low temperature, around 65° C., some polymerization

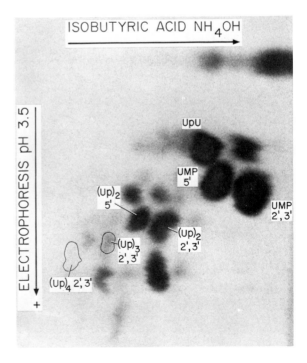

A nucleoside (a sugar joined to a base, in this case uracil+ribose) has been heated with an inorganic phosphate, to simulate what may have happened in a dried up ocean. Paper chromatography, using radioactive labelled materials, has enabled us to locate the first stages of polymerization. Dinucleotides have been formed

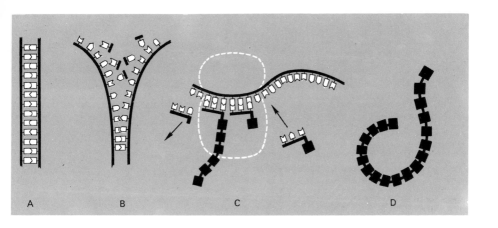

A   B   C   D

appears to take place. In these thermal experiments, which simulate conditions in which water is absent, the phosphates used were generally orthophosphates. It has been shown that the mechanisms of these phosphorylations may have been due to the formation of linear phosphates. On being heated, the orthophosphates become polyphosphates, and these polyphosphates are responsible for the synthesis of macromolecules.

While exploring the pathway for the direct synthesis of polypeptides and polynucleotides, we must look for mechanisms by which correlations between amino acids and nucleotides may have taken place in the primordial ocean. Today we know that the relationship between the nucleic acid and the protein is fundamental, and that there are processes for the transfer of information from a nucleic acid molecule to a protein molecule. The interaction between the individual components, or polymers, must have taken place very early in the course of chemical evolution. The study of these interconnections would help us to understand the origin of the genetic code which some biochemists consider synonymous with the origin of life.

The transfer of information from the cell nucleus to the main body of the cell, directing the making of protein by means of the 'code' spelt out along the DNA molecule, is the fundamental process of life. It must have evolved over an immense period of time from simple self-replicatory mechanisms in the first macromolecules. The process starts (A–B) with the making of a molecule of ribonucleic acid (RNA), matching, step by step, the 'template' provided by one strand of the DNA helix. The RNA 'messenger' molecules leave the nucleus and fix themselves to the ribosomes (C), minute bodies in the cell fluid which are rich in a soluble RNA, the so-called 'transfer' RNA. This RNA collects amino acids from the cell fluid, transfers them to the ribosomes, and delivers them to the messenger molecule at the precise place where its three-unit backbone of bases fits on. The peptide bond (p. 86) links the amino acids together to form the protein chain (D) and complete the simple sequence

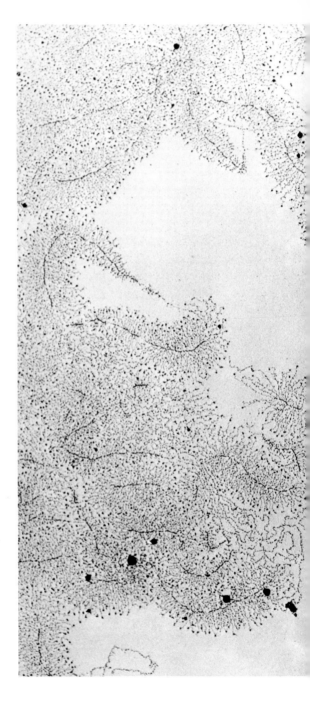

This historic electron micrograph (about 24,000 times magnification) shows, for the first time, the production of ribonucleic acid in the process pictured in the preceding diagram. Linked together like beads on a necklace (the string being the DNA molecule), the genes – the carrot-shaped structures in the picture – are each giving off about 100 hair-like molecules of RNA. This is a vivid illustration of the complexity of the operations that can take place in a single cell

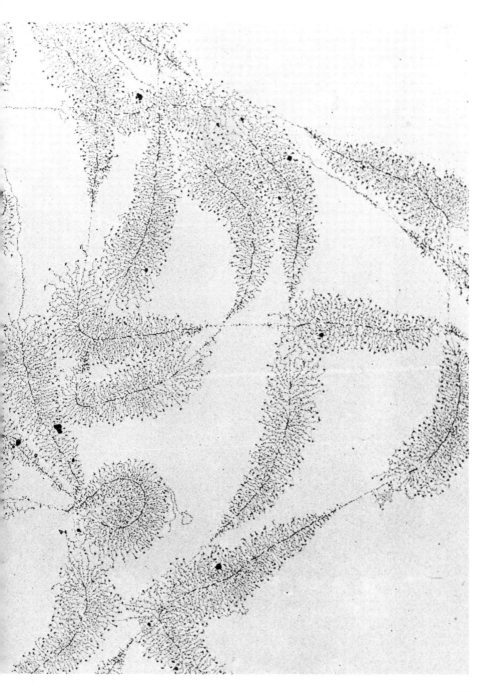

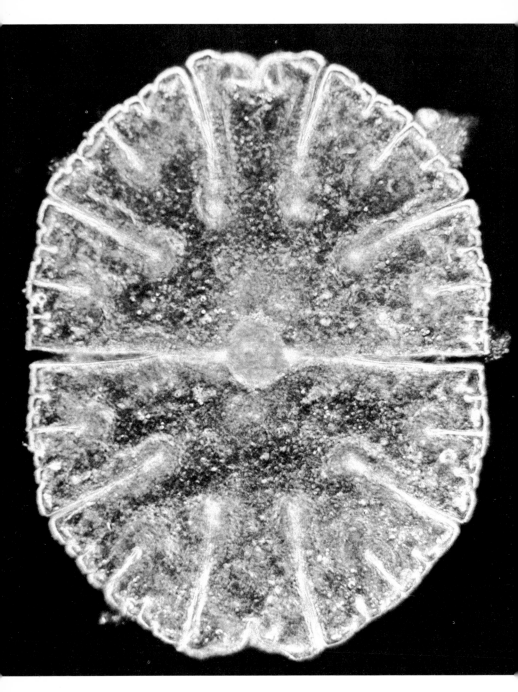

PROTOCELLS   8

The cell is the basic unit of life. Unicellular organisms occupy a conspicuous place at the base of the
evolutionary tree. Although biochemically it is
conceivable that the phenomena of growth and
replication associated with living processes may be
exhibited at the macromolecular level, there is a
strong tendency to place the cell at the centre of
biology. It is important therefore to consider
whether some rudimentary forms, which later
blossomed into the structural units of plant and
animal life, were already in existence in the prebiotic era. Several models have been presented to
illustrate the origin of the first cell in the twilight
period of transition from chemistry to biology.

Chief among these are the coacervates, small
colloidal inclusions with osmotic properties. These
droplets are called coacervates from the Latin
coacervare, meaning to assemble together or cluster
together. The possibility of building up such high-
molecular-weight compounds from dilute fluids
was described by the Dutch chemist Bungenberg de
Jong in his studies of colloidal solutions. Oparin
applied these ideas to organic molecules in the
context of chemical evolution.

The plausibility of these drops as models of
prebiological systems derives from the fact that

*Evolved over millions of years, the
Micrasterias* alga *(opposite,* ×
*1,000) is still a one-celled organism,
as the first living things were*

they form readily in extremely weak solutions. The aggregation of molecules is a result of the action between opposite electrical charges. Small spherules are formed because water molecules assemble in a sheet around accumulating polymers. Within the ensemble, further molecular interaction takes place until the drops become larger. Coacervate formation not only serves as a method of providing a locally segregated environment distinguished by a boundary from the exterior, but also permits the matrix within the structure to interact with the external environment. The permeable walls permit a passage of material from the outside to the inside, and vice versa, on a selective basis. The demarcation from the surrounding medium allows the individual units to acquire a very high degree of specificity. This could be a spontaneous effect under ideal conditions.

Oparin and his associates have prepared coacervate droplets from a large number of different biological compounds. Perhaps their most significant experiments relate to the function of enzymes within these 'precells'. In some instances, enzymatic reactions have been shown to have taken place within or on the walls of the coacervate. At this stage, we do not have sufficient information to conclude that coacervation was the way in which the first cells came into being. However, the flexibility of their structures, their ease of formation, and their ability to concentrate small molecules in extremely dilute solutions possibly give coacervates a unique role in precellular evolution.

The first cells?

Fox has proposed microspheres as a conceivable pathway by which the first cells may have appeared on the earth. They are little hard spheres made from proteinoids which, in turn, are synthesized when

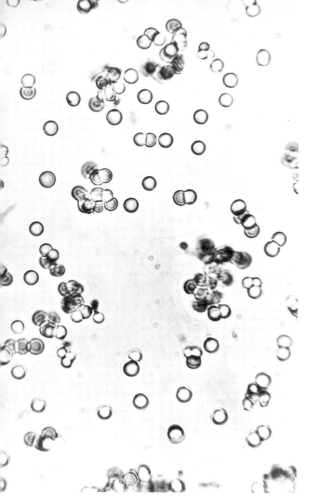

When polymers of amino acids are heated, dissolved in boiling water and allowed to cool, they tend to form these tiny spheres, about two thousandths of a millimetre across. This has been suggested as a way in which the precursors of the living, self-replicating cell appeared

amino acids are heated to about 180° C. These polymers of amino acids dissolve in boiling water and, on cooling, give rise to large numbers of minute spherules. A single milligram of proteinoid may give as many as 100 million microspheres. Each one of these is not more than about 2 microns in diameter, and they have often been compared to bacteria in shape and size. They can be washed with salt solutions and cut into sections in which the outer walls appear to have a double layer. In some instances, bud-like structures have been formed.

Although microspheres are interesting objects of study, there is no way of establishing that they are the ancestors of the first cells. The sequence of events leading to their formation inclines one to believe that they may not have been of very common occurrence on the primitive earth. An environment where thermal energy was commonplace would have been an essential prerequisite for the appearance of microspheres.

Many other methods and procedures may be cited as illustrations of the manner in which a primordial cell appeared on earth. For example, the occurrence of biphasic vesicles at the boundary of the oceans is an appealing feature. If there was a film of lipids, or a layer of hydrocarbons on the surface of the ancient seas, the action of wind and wave could have separated small rounded globules in this membrane. Organic matter in the oceans would have been included in the bubbles thus generated. Interaction within these spheres would have constituted the birth of biochemistry.

Recent calculations made by Holland, the Princeton geologist, have shown that if ultraviolet light acted upon the methane of the earth's primitive atmosphere, hydrocarbons would have accumulated on the early oceans. According to him, the oil slick which would have been generated by such a process may have been several metres deep. It is reasonable to believe that membranes may have been formed long before the processes which they were destined to protect were in existence.

There is an extensive literature dealing with the accumulation of various solutions of organic matter and the resulting cell-like structures. However, the leap from morphology to function is fraught with danger, especially when we consider entities of several billion years ago.

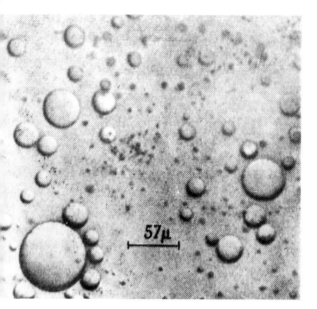

57μ

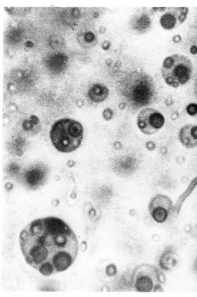

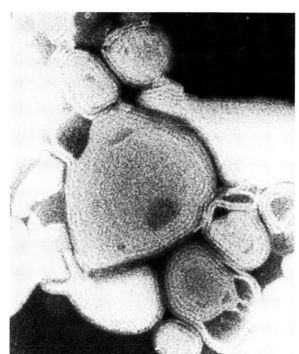

All conjecture about how the first cell-like structures could have arisen is highly speculative. This is the misty borderland between chemistry and biology, where there have been many explorers but few firm answers. Above, left: coacervate (clustering) droplets spontaneously formed by the interaction between gelatine and gum arabic. Above: similar droplets containing chlorophyll. Left: a group of chemical compounds called phospholipids can be seen (under the electron microscope) to form multi-layered structures resembling the myelin sheath that encloses animal nerve cells

RIGHT-HANDED AND LEFT-HANDED MOLECULES

9

We have grown accustomed to learning chemistry from two-dimensional formulae but, in reality, there is a profound difference in the shapes of molecules. Like the right and left hands, some molecules are mirror images of each other. Chemically, these molecules are identical but, by virtue of their structural difference, they appear as opposites. In some instances, the asymmetric character is manifested in the shape of the crystals. A hundred years ago, Louis Pasteur, with the aid of a high-powered lens, separated the right-handed and left-handed crystals of sodium ammonium tartarate. Although this method of separation is limited to a very few cases, Pasteur's discovery was of great theoretical importance. Since solutions of these crystals deflected a beam of polarized light in opposite directions, he related this optical activity to the geometrical structure of the molecule.

Pasteur was also the first to observe that the molecules related to life were asymmetric in configuration. The amino acids found in proteins of living organisms are all levorotatory or L-amino acids, and the sugars are dextrorotatory or D-

Opposite: the 'handedness' of nature shows up even in the spiral growth patterns of polymethylene crystals. At a magnification of 37,000 times it can be seen that some crystals grow in a clockwise direction, some anti-clockwise

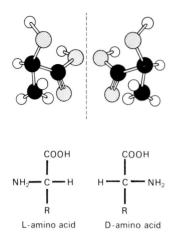

COOH
|
NH$_2$—C—H
|
R

L-amino acid

COOH
|
H—C—NH$_2$
|
R

D-amino acid

Mirror images of each other, like right-hand and left-hand gloves, the two forms of lactic acid (model, top) are chemically identical, and distinguished only by the opposite ways in which a solution of their crystals rotates a beam of polarized light. Similarly an amino acid (above) may have an L-form (left-ward twist), or a D-form which is otherwise identical

sugars, i.e., the beam of polarized light we discussed earlier is deflected to the left in one instance and to the right in the other. Outside the living world, everything is racemic, which means that it consists of equal amounts of the right-handed and left-handed molecules. But, in living organisms, only one form is used. Although there are traces of D-amino acids on the cell walls of certain bacteria, in general the molecular make-up of the living organism is principally asymmetric in nature. Indeed, this specific feature has led many to believe that the presence of optical activity is an infallible criterion of life.

Why do the proteins in living organisms make use only of the left-handed amino acids? Perhaps the choice was made a long time ago, and any attempt to tamper with it would have been like trying to put a right shoe on the left foot. It is intriguing to speculate how the selection first occurred. Did the preference evolve before life began? Did most of the molecules that were synthesized on the primordial earth consist only of one form? These are questions that remain unanswered.

Crystals of sodium ammonium tartarate, and enlarged model crystals. With this compound Pasteur discovered the asymmetric structure of the crystals, and with the models he illustrated his lectures on this discovery

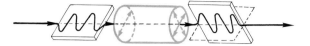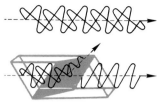

The most prevalent type of configuration assumed by proteins is the alpha-helix. This is a coiled structure which resembles a rod rather than a tube. Polypeptides assume this structure spontaneously on account of their inherent dynamic stability. Laboratory experiments to synthesize polypeptides from mixtures of left- and right-handed molecules have met with complete failure because of the inability of the molecular shapes to fit into each other without imposing a strain on the chemical bonds. Thus, a helix grows very rapidly when the compounds are in one optically active form or the other and polypeptides composed of a single form appear to have an enormous advantage. There is a tendency to segregate left- and right-handed forms, and this requirement becomes even more rigorous as the proteins become larger and more complex.

A similar pattern is observed in the case of the nucleic acids. The Watson and Crick structure of

Light waves normally vibrate in any of an infinity of planes around their line of travel: they are 'incoherent'. Passage through or reflection from certain substances filters out all the waves except those vibrating in one plane (above); the light is now 'polarized'. Sometimes polarized light can pass into a substance and come out with its plane of polarization rotated to the left or right (above, left). A substance with this property is said to be 'optically active'

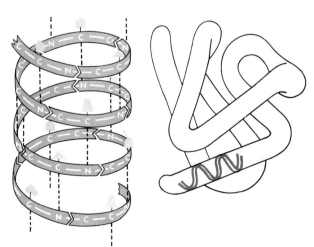

The most usual shape of a protein molecule is a helix (far left). The carbon-carbon-nitrogen sequence along the backbone is so spaced, and so held together by hydrogen bonds between the amino acids, that a left-handed helix is the only stable form it can adopt. It might have been right-handed but nature happened to 'choose' left. Even in the complex secondary folding (left) of the helix which is the true shape of the protein molecule, individual to each kind, the left-hand thread remains

the DNA molecule depends on the arrangement of various functional groups about the asymmetric carbon atom of the sugar, deoxyribose. In the nucleotides, the purine and pyrimidine bases always have the same orientation towards the sugar molecule, and a right-handed helix results. A choice of molecules of opposite stereochemistry led to a stable, but different, structure. The nature of the choice is therefore critical. As in the case of the proteins, the use of one isomer is essential for the stability of the aggregate of molecules making up the nucleic acid chain. But this still does not explain why L-amino acids are required for sound and sturdy proteins, or why the D-configuration of deoxyribose is essential for a viable double helix of DNA.

If it is assumed that life began as the result of a single isolated event upon the earth, there would be no problem in attributing the beginnings of molecular chirality ('handedness') to the left-handedness or right-handedness of the initial molecules chosen. The evidence which has accumulated to date favours the idea that the origin of life was of general occurrence in numberless sites on earth. If the molecules required for life were already present, it could be argued that there was a greater abundance of L-amino acids and D-sugars under primordial conditions. Many suggestions have been made for the preferential synthesis of one form over the other. One of the earliest concerns the use of circularly polarized light, emanating from the moon or accompanying the reflection of solar light from the oceans. The magnetic field of the earth may have also influenced the polarization of light in such a manner. In spite of the apparent plausibility of this pathway, there is very little experimental evidence which can be marshalled in its support.

Asymmetric surfaces also may have played a role

in the generation of one form preferentially. Quartz crystals of left-handed, or right-handed, form may have been the surface on which early synthesis took place. The left-handed quartz forms would, no doubt, induce L-amino acids, while the right-handed ones would give rise to D-amino acids. However, under natural conditions, there are equal amounts of both types of crystals. Once again, the same question appears in a different guise.

The seeding of racemic mixtures has been proposed as an answer to the problem of the origin of optical activity. If, in spontaneous crystallization, the first crystal to appear happened to be left-handed it is likely that more left-handed crystals

James Watson (left) and Francis Crick, with their first model of the DNA molecule – supreme example of a molecule with a right-handed twist

would have been generated. Experiments performed by organic chemists have shown that seeding can, indeed, result in the dominance of one form over the other. However, if crystallization of the original nuclei took place in random fashion, there should have been equal numbers of instances involving both L-amino acids and D-amino acids. So far, the results of experiments on asymmetric synthesis do not seem to help us in answering the question.

We may conclude by saying that the original choice was, in a sense, arbitrary. Both forms, left-handed and right-handed, appeared as a result of prebiological synthesis. In the early struggle for existence, both forms were employed. There would have been two populations of polymers, some that were right-handed, and some that were left-handed. As organisms began to live on other organisms, it would have become highly advantageous for these early creatures to use a single

The electron carries a negative charge; its anti-particle the positron carries an equal and opposite positive charge – made visible in this cloud chamber photograph by means of a magnetic field. As it speeds through the cloud chamber the particle veers left or right according to its charge – but negative and positive charge are symmetrical in physics, unlike the left- and right-handedness of organic life

configuration. The ordinary pressures of selection would have quickly forced one or other of the forms from this planet. If the choice is arbitrary, the survey of life in the universe should reveal to us approximately equal numbers of populations with L- and D-amino acids. If one could sample all the different organisms of all habitable planets, there would, perhaps, be equal numbers of left-handed and right-handed molecules.

George Wald of Harvard once asked Einstein about this problem and he replied: 'You know, I used to wonder how it comes about that the electron is negative. Negative – positive – these are perfectly symmetric in physics. There is no reason whatever to prefer one to the other. Then why is the electron negative? I thought about this a long time, and at last all I could think was "It won in the fight!"' To which responded Wald: 'That's just what I think of the L-amino acids. They won in the fight!'

THE FITNESS OF CARBON

10

In the synthesis described so far, we have assumed that carbon atoms were essential for life. Is carbon the only basis for life? Organic matter is made up chiefly of carbon, hydrogen, nitrogen, and oxygen. Phosphorus and sulphur participate to a limited extent. There are also the monatomic ions of the elements – sodium, potassium, magnesium, calcium and chlorine. Iron, manganese, cobalt, copper and zinc are also found as trace metals, binding metallo-organic complexes.

Apart from helium, the lighter elements are most abundant in the universe. One reason for their use in living systems may be attributed to their availability. In a recent paper, George Wald has described other crucial factors which influenced their selection, in particular their fitness, or peculiar combination of properties that would make a particular element ideally suited for its function in biomolecules.

We might first pose the question, why hydrogen, oxygen, nitrogen, and carbon? Besides being preponderant under cosmic conditions they are the smallest elements in the periodic table. They can achieve the electronic configuration of the nearest inert gases by the addition of one, two, three, or

Opposite: diamond is pure carbon. Each atom bonds to four others in a stable lattice whose geometry is mirrored in the crystal shape and whose stability is shown by the diamond's unrivalled hardness

	K shell		K shell	L shell		K shell	L shell	M shell		K shell	L shell	M shell	N shell
		lithium Li	2	1	sodium Na	2	8	1	potassium K	2	8	8	1
		beryllium Be	2	2	magnesium Mg	2	8	2	calcium Ca	2	8	8	2
									(the ten transition metals)				
		boron B	2	3	aluminium Al	2	8	3	gallium Ga	2	8	18	3
hydrogen H	1	carbon C	2	4	silicon Si	2	8	4	germanium Ge	2	8	18	4
		nitrogen N	2	5	phosphorus P	2	8	5	arsenic As	2	8	18	5
		oxygen O	2	6	sulphur S	2	8	6	selenium Se	2	8	18	6
		fluorine F	2	7	chlorine Cl	2	8	7	bromine Br	2	8	18	7
helium He	2	neon Ne	2	8	argon Ar	2	8	8	krypton Kr	2	8	18	8

The periodic table. Picked out in grey are the four elements all-important to life – or at any rate to life as it has developed on this planet

four electrons. In other words, by the addition of electrons, stability is readily obtained. The atoms of carbon, hydrogen, and nitrogen are also small in size. These two factors invest the atoms of these elements with the capacity of forming stable and multiple bonds. In the process of ordinary bond formation, there is a sharing of electrons. In some instances, however, more than one electron can be involved, and a multiple bond is formed. This is very important in biological processes since it gives the atom great flexibility, and versatility, to combine with a number of other atoms.

When carbon is considered in opposition to silicon, we see that, on earth, silicon is more plentiful than carbon. As a matter of fact, there is 135 times more silicon than carbon. Carbon can gain four electrons, and form four covalent bonds.

Silicon can also do the same. Why, then, is life based upon carbon instead of on silicon? The answer seems to be that the carbon-carbon bond, at 80 kilocalories per mole, has nearly twice the stability of the silicon–silicon bond, which is only 42 kilocalories. In the business of making tight and stable bonds, carbon thus appears to have an intrinsic advantage.

The manner in which carbon is combined with oxygen offers another point of comparison. Carbon can combine with oxygen to give rise to the molecule carbon dioxide, a gas which is free to associate with many other compounds. Silicon dioxide, on the other hand, is quartz. When silicon combines with oxygen, the unpaired electrons of the silicon atom link up with the neighbouring oxygen atoms, generating the huge super-molecule of silicon

Crystals of quartz – silicon dioxide. Unlike carbon dioxide, it cannot interact with other molecules

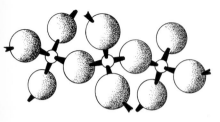

When silicon (small sphere) combines with oxygen it forms silicon dioxide, or quartz. As silicon has a valency of four, and oxygen of two, all valency requirements are satisfied and no further interactions can take place

The arrangement of electrons in shells around the nucleus is superficially similar in carbon and silicon. But though each has four electrons in the outermost shell, and thus a valency of four, silicon's empty outer sub-shell makes for weaker bonding. In spite of silicon's much greater abundance, carbon bonds more readily and strongly with other elements, and so is the basic element of life. Carbon chemistry is organic chemistry

dioxide in the form of quartz. This immediately removes the silicon from circulation. Besides, the unwieldy large crystals cannot interact with other molecules.

The bond between silicon atoms is weak and susceptible to attack by various reagents, such as water or ammonia. It is unlikely that the long chains required for the macromolecules of life would have been formed by the use of silicon. This is evident from a consideration of the distribution of electrons in the silicon and carbon atoms. There are several levels at which the electrons around the nucleus of an atom are distributed. Where the carbon atom is concerned, we are dealing with electrons in the second energy level which has two sub-levels, called the *s* and *p* orbitals. There is an interaction, or hybridization, between these two orbitals. In the case of the silicon atom, however, the bonding electrons are at the third energy level, where there are three sub-levels – *s*, *p* and *d* orbitals. Even though the four combining, or valence, electrons occupy the *s* and *p* levels, the vacant *d* orbital is an invitation for an invasion by free electrons of neighbouring atoms.

We might summarize the reasons why silicon has not been implicated in biological molecules by saying, first of all, that silicon atoms form bonds

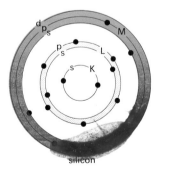

silicon

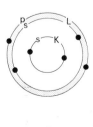

carbon

which are much weaker than carbon–carbon bonds. There is also a reluctance on the part of silicon to form multiple bonds. On account of this, it becomes unavailable for further involvement with the environment. In addition, the chains of this element are unstable in the presence of water and ammonia. It is a fact of experience that, in spite of its abundance on earth, no silicon has been incorporated into any functional molecule or been enlisted in the service of metabolic activity.

Many of the molecules that are essential to living systems exhibit a mobility and fluidity in the composition and make-up of their chemical bonds. This phenomenon is aptly described as the 'delocalization' of the electrons, implying that the electrons are not rigidly constrained to a certain geometric configuration. In the structure of such molecules as the nucleic acids, proteins, energy-rich phosphates and enzymes, the electrons are assumed to be present as a diffuse cloud around the backbone,

Carbon forms stable and multiple bonds, either in the pure state or in compounds. One form of pure carbon (above), less strong than the other, diamond, is the black graphite of lead pencils

117

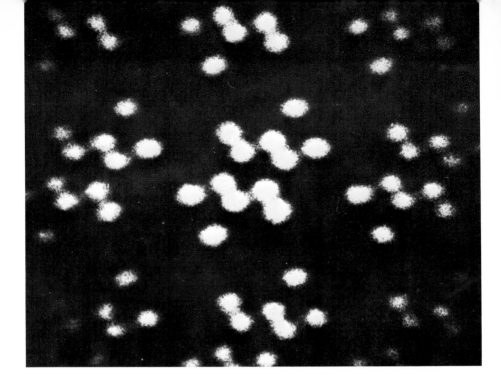

Six carbon atoms in a ring – the benzene ring. The hexagonal arrangement of the atoms in the molecule (though not the atoms themselves) can now be made visible by a process based on X-ray diffraction

as in the case of the benzene ring. According to the French theoretical chemists Bernard and Alberte Pullman, this phenomenon, in which the electrons are more mobile, seems to have made an important contribution to the origin and evolution of life.

What are the benefits of delocalization to those compounds which are the principal building blocks of living matter? Two answers suggest themselves. Firstly, these molecules become much more stable because of the way in which the electrons are distributed along their backbone. Secondly, the major result of this distribution of electrons is a gain in energy – what the chemist calls 'resonance energy'. The structures are described as 'resonating' between different forms, and an unexpected economy results. For example, in the biosynthesis of adenine, the resonance energy available is about 50 to 60 kilocalories per mole, which is the amount of energy required for the build-up of this purine. The gain appears to be offset by the expenditure of energy. The net result is stability.

This kind of permanence must have played a very important part in the early selection of molecules during the period of chemical evolution, an epoch in which there must have been some struggle for their survival. It is confirmed by the extraordinary unity of biochemistry. The same limited number of compounds are used over and over again in the plant and animal kingdom. The case of adenine is most obvious. Adenine is found in the two nucleic acids. In addition, it is a constituent of adenosine triphosphate (ATP), the energy source of all living systems, and of the co-enzymes, those small 'helper' molecules without which some enzymes cannot perform their catalytic functions. An examination of its structure firmly establishes the fact that it is the most stable of the purines.

These molecules are also able to resist radiation. This is a distinct advantage since the molecules that were formed by ultraviolet light, ionizing radiation, or electrical discharges had to survive in order to interact with each other to form the giant polymers necessary for life. They must have been able to shield themselves from the radiation effects. Further, their resonance energy gives them an ascendancy in the production of larger molecules.

The quantum chemical consideration of biomolecules leads to the following very pertinent conclusions. In the early stages of evolution and selection, the sturdiest compounds were used. It was, in fact, their resonance energy which enabled them to survive long enough to be selected for this purpose. Further, these molecules, because of the property of delocalization, were best adapted for biological purposes. Life did not originate with the appearance of these systems, but we might say that their appearance made it more probable.

MOLECULAR FOSSILS 11

The fossil record on earth may harbour some of the secrets of our earlier beginnings. Stones, rocks, and sediments may conceal the long-drawn-out story of terrestrial life.

The geological 'clock' overleaf represents the age of the earth on a twelve-hour face. It is a sobering thought that on this clock the life of man is less than a minute in extent. The evolutionary process took a prodigious amount of time to develop from the very first organism to the advanced forms with which we are familiar today.

The dark line at around six hundred million years ago represents the base of the Cambrian. There was a time when paleontologists thought that no life existed beyond this period as no skeletons had been unearthed older than six hundred million years. Although much of the geological history of the earth transpired in the Precambrian era, little effort had been made to examine the rocks and sediments of this very ancient epoch. The greatest activity has centred around more recent geological times. However, the student of chemical evolution is more interested in the remote past. The painstaking efforts of the micropaleontologists Barghoorn and Schopf have shown us that life was already in

Opposite: the billion-year-old rocks of Bitter Springs, in the Northern Territory of Australia

existence over three billion years ago. When the transition took place from the early atmosphere, reducing in nature, to the oxygen-laden atmosphere that we have today, life had already begun and was undergoing a slow process of evolution.

Several rock formations bear silent testimony to the cataclysmic changes which must have taken place through the aeons of geological time. At one billion years, there exists the Bitter Springs terrain

The clock face of geological time. Man appeared at one minute to twelve

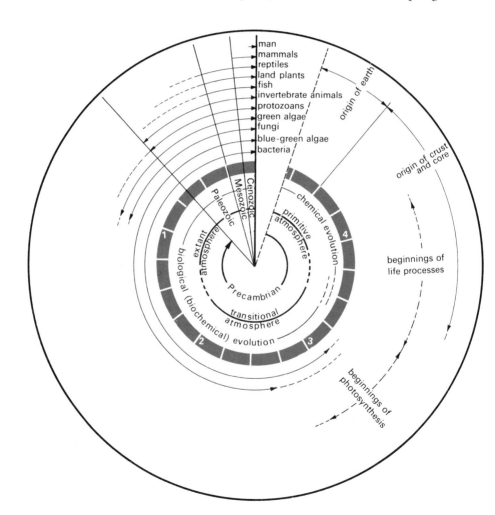

of the Northern Territory of Australia. Back another billion years, we come to an outcrop found, this time, in the north-eastern part of the United States and south-eastern Canada – the Gunflint Chert of Ontario. Some of the surface rocks of this deposit protrude into Lake Ontario. The Soudan obtrusion at 2.9 billion years, also found in North America in the Minnesota and Montana area, takes us well into the early Precambrian. Of paramount interest are the rocks of the Fig Tree and Onverwacht series of South Africa. The Fig Tree, dated at 3.1 billion, derives its name from the town of Fig Tree in Barberton. Underlying this is the Onverwacht Shale, thought to be about 3.4 to 3.6 billion years old. Some geologists believe that the oldest sedimentary rocks on the earth may be found here. The earth's original crust may have been buried by mountain-building activity, and thus may be for ever beyond our reach.

Precambrian paleobiology is a recent science, and advances have been made only in the last few years. Among the different microorganisms, or microfossils, that have been identified in these rocks and sediments, there are fewer than three dozen which are well preserved and suitable for study. Fortunately, the earliest deposits have provided an ideal geological setting for the preservation of the structure of these delicate microorganisms. It is to be expected that the structures that have been found unimpaired in cherts are not representative of the total flora and fauna of the time.

As we journey backwards into the Precambrian period, the first evidence for life is found in the microflora of Bitter Springs from Australia. It is about 900 million years old, and microfossils are extremely well preserved in their diversity. This particular deposit has been reported by Barghoorn and Schopf to contain about 30 different species.

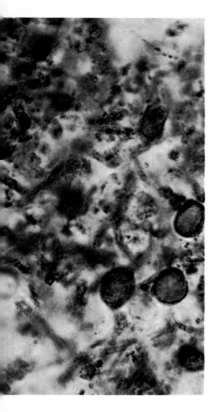

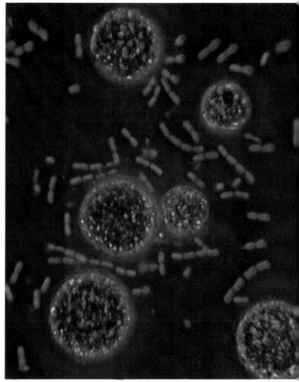

Fossil algae from the Gunflint chert, Canada (left), two billion years old, show some morphological similarity to algae living today (right, × 1,500). Between and around the living algae are thread-like assemblages of bacteria

Barghoorn and Schopf's electron microscopic studies of shape, form and structure have revealed what appear to be blue-green algae, possibly red algae, and even some fungi. It is noteworthy that, of the 19 species of blue-green algae which are apparent in Bitter Springs, 14 may be similar in structure to modern types of algae. At least six or seven of them are comparable to living algae. Thus, some of the most ancient species found on earth seem to have been preserved as living fossils in the biosphere of today. The morphology of these fossils is varied, diverse, and highly structured, implying that they had reached a very high degree of organization. Comparing these organisms with those found today provides us with one of the most

striking examples of conservatism in evolutionary development.

The Gunflint iron formation is thought to be about 1.6 to 2 billion years old. The rocks are found at a latitude which passes along the northern shore of Lake Superior in Ontario. In lateral extent, it is about 150 miles, and varies from a few inches to about two feet in thickness. The intact microfossils are composed predominantly of algae. The deposits consist of laminar mats near the interface between sediments and the water of the shallow basins. The cells, entrapped and embedded in rapidly deposited colloidal silica, were filled in the process and the cell walls have been left intact, or have been preserved by lithification. In this assemblage,

Typical Gunflint chert territory, four miles west of Schreiber, Ontario, on the shore of Lake Superior: among the oldest rocks on the surface of the earth

twelve species of microscopic plants have been recognized. Most of these are unicellular and spheroidal. The variation in size and surface texture of these microfossils indicates that several species are represented. Some forms may be related to filamentous bacteria, which appear among species about two billion years old from the Witwatersrand group of South Africa.

An unusual structure identified in the Gunflint is *Kakabekia umbellata*, which consists of an umbrella-like cap, basal bulb, and slender connecting stalk. In one of the samples examined, Barghoorn and Tyler were able to arrange a series of microfossils in possible sequence of individual development. During the development of what may be interpreted as the adult form, the bulb decreases in size, giving rise to a corresponding increase in the umbrella-like cap. There has been some speculation about the recent discovery made by Siegel of a

The strange umbrella-like shape of Kakabekia umbellata, which flourished in an ammonia-rich atmosphere in the Pre-Cambrian era

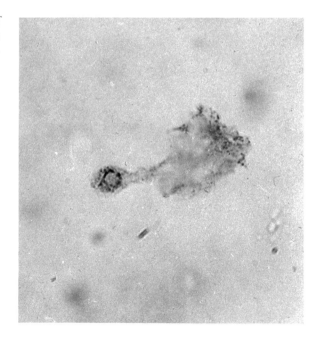

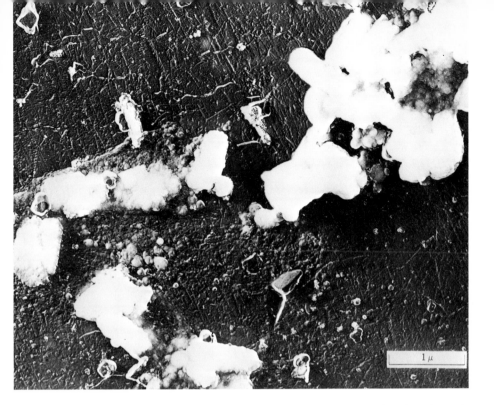

specimen very similar in shape and form to *Kakabekia umbellata* in some sand taken from near the walls of Harlech Castle in Wales. It has been suggested that this organism lived in an ammonia-rich environment and survives today in a niche recapturing the conditions in which it flourished in the early Precambrian era. This evidence is only from morphology, and will have to be further substantiated by the examination of the structure and chemical composition of *Kakabekia*.

The electron microscopic studies of the Gunflint have shown some rod-shaped bacteria. On comparison with microorganisms which are found today, it is likely that these rods may be related to the modern iron bacteria. The occurrence of these structures may denote that iron-bearing layers may have been deposited as a result of the biologic activity of these organisms.

From the Gunflint chert of Canada come these fossil bacteria, their shapes clearly revealed by etching and shadowing. Morphologically similar to certain iron bacteria of today, they are among the most ancient fossils now known

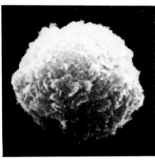

Top: thread-like filament of organic matter from the Fig Tree chert of Southern Africa, over three thousand million years old. From the Onverwacht group of rocks in Swaziland, which are even older than the Fig Tree chert, come organized microstructures like this (above, shown at a magnification of × 1,400) – perhaps the remains of the oldest living thing yet identified

Barghoorn, Schopf, Engels, and others have unearthed what may very well be the oldest known microfossils in the South African cherts. The Fig Tree chert has yielded the most intriguing bacteria-like microfossils. They are organically preserved in the black cherts dated at around 3.1 billion years. The physiological characteristics of these minute, rod-shaped structures are very uncertain, but their size, shape, cell wall, and ultrastructure have been displayed in electron microscopic studies. The micropaleontologist is inclined to think that the general morphology of these structures is similar to that of the modern blue-green algae. Is it possible that some of these microorganisms could have been photosynthetic autotrophs? Photosynthesis may have been already at work in these very early stages. In the lower regions of the Swaziland group are rocks older than the Fig Tree chert. They have been called the Onverwacht group, meaning, literally, 'unexpected'. Recently, it has been reported that microstructures, resembling those found in the Fig Tree chert, have been identified in this formation. Indeed, these microfossils would then appear to be the remains of the oldest living entities identified upon the earth.

The microfossil evidence would lead us to suppose that biological systems originated during the very earliest period of geological time, probably between $4\frac{1}{4}$ and $3\frac{1}{2}$ billion years ago. If the microstructures found in the Fig Tree and Onverwacht cherts are indeed as complex as they appear to be in their fossilized form, a great deal of time may have been required for them to evolve to this point. In our discussion of the synthesis of organic compounds and primitive atmospheres, it was maintained that the early atmosphere was reducing in nature. If the algae appeared in the primordial oceans around $3\frac{1}{2}$ billion years ago, photosynthesis must already have been at work, and the atmosphere must have changed gradually from a reducing to an anoxic one and, finally, to the oxygenic environment of the Paleozoic era.

We might conclude that the early Precambrian life-forms were, indeed, quite primitive. They occurred as isolated cells, and it is only with the evolution of the filamentous forms that they began to be found in communities. During the middle Precambrian, however, planktonic algae were perhaps very abundant locally. The blue-green

Section of chalk showing micro-fossils (× 165) similar to blue-green algae. By the middle Pre-Cambrian, some two billion years ago, photo-synthetic organisms such as these must have been widespread

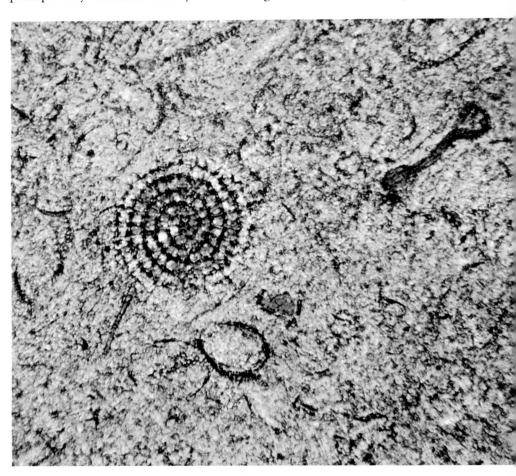

algae and a host of other chemosynthetic bacteria may have appeared. It is assumed that photosynthetic microorganisms were widespread during this time and that the oxygenic atmosphere had begun to develop at this juncture. In the late Precambrian age, there may have been an assemblage of organisms morphologically comparable to those that we see today. The blue-green algae, for example, may have reached a high degree of diversification in their development. At this point, perhaps, the cell with an enclosed nucleus may have already arrived on the scene. This event may be regarded as a noteworthy development, heralding the dawn of cell duplication, and the origin of diversification.

Fossil chemicals

There is yet another fossil that one could scrutinize – the molecular, or chemical, fossil. The examination of ancient rocks and sediments has brought to light minute quantities of organic compounds which may be traced back to the sources from whence they came. While the organism itself may have been destroyed, the molecules that were embodied in this structure have survived in these rocks. In the study of modern organic geochemistry, some of the molecules related to life are being isolated from these ancient rocks and sediments.

The German chemist Treibs first extracted metal-containing porphyrins from crude oils, and thus established that the study of individual molecules in a geochemical setting might be useful in disclosing the nature of the organisms living at the time the organic matter may have been deposited. Since porphyrins are important in biological processes, Treibs's identification of them led him to conclude that oils were biological in origin.

The great concern about the analysis of extra-terrestrial samples has kindled a new interest in organic geochemistry. A simple laboratory technique for such work requires, first of all, the selection of a suitable sediment so that the piece of chert or rock which is massive in character can be isolated. There should be no cracks or crevices into which recent organic matter may have seeped. A piece of the chert is carefully removed to avoid gross contamination from the outside, is then pulverized, and extracted with organic solvents. In such a process, it is customary to treat the rock with a variety of solvents. Some of the molecules, such as sugars and amino acids, can be extracted with water. Hydrocarbons and porphyrins may be removed by benzene and methane. Further reaction of the pulverized rock with acid might release other organic compounds which could not have been extracted by direct treatment with the solvents.

In his search, the chemist first focuses his attention on those molecules which are related to life. However, not all of these may be suitable for his purpose since the chances of their preservation over long periods of time may turn out to be small. The hydrocarbons constitute a useful category for examination. Because they tend to resist the natural processes of dissolution and recombination they may be markers of the kind of chemistry that existed at the time that they were deposited. The organic matter available for analysis from such a procedure of extraction and hydrolysis may have originated from a variety of organisms. They underwent a metamorphosis from the form in which they existed in the living creatures.

The normal alkanes, or straight-chain hydro-carbons, are commonly found in biological systems today. The odd-carbon numbers appear to be more abundant. These two factors may be used as biological markers. The predominance of the odd-carbon over the even is a result of the decarboxylation of the lipids to the hydrocarbons. Even-numbered fatty acids lose a single carbon atom and give rise to an odd-carbon, straight-chain alkane. Along with the normal alkanes, it is useful to look for the isoprenoids, pristane and phytane. The side chain of the chlorophyll molecule, the 20-carbon segment which hangs like a tail from one end of the porphyrin molecule, can be broken down to these two isoprenoids. The presence of pristane and phytane has been considered to be indicative of photosynthesis.

In searching for these hydrocarbons, the extracted lipid fraction can be treated with a molecular sieve. This is a device which consists of many small hollow spherules of a cross-linked polymer such as dextran. The spaces between the cross-linkages act as holes in the walls of the hollow spherules, allowing straight-chain hydrocarbons to enter but excluding branched-chain molecules such as the isoprenoids. The sieve is then washed with the solvent which will now contain the isoprenoids. The alkanes are firmly entrenched inside the sieve. By dissolving the sieve material in acid, the hydrocarbons can be released. Gas chromatography discloses the identity of these compounds.

By such methods, the normal alkanes and isoprenoids have been located in the ancient Precambrian rocks all the way back to the Onverwacht shale. Similar results have been achieved in the quest for the porphyrin molecule. With the aid of the fluorescence assay technique, it has been clearly demonstrated that porphyrins have been found in the 3.4-billion-year-old rocks.

An exhaustive search has been made for the presence of amino acids. Most of the amino acids

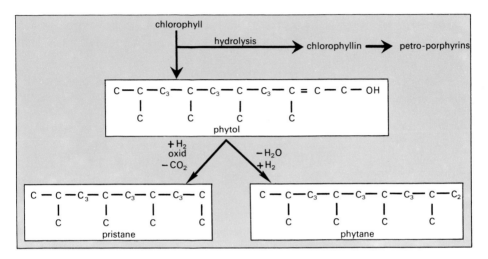

Among 'chemical fossils', straight-chain hydrocarbons are useful indicators of biological material; they are formed from fatty acids (top) by the removal of a carbon atom as CO_2. Pristane and phytane (centre), breakdown products of the chlorophyll molecule's 20-carbon tail (above), are probably indicators of photosynthesis

found in the ancient rocks have been of the L form, not unlike those found in modern organisms. After a certain period of time, perhaps about 60 million years, left-handed and right-handed forms tend to become equally prevalent. These results have therefore been interpreted to mean that the organic matter in ancient rocks may be of recent origin.

Are they signs of life?

One of the most vexing problems in the field of organic geochemistry is the difficulty of judging whether the molecules identified are abiogenic or biological in origin. Unambiguous criteria of biogenicity are critical. Although the biological markers, such as normal alkanes, isoprenoids, porphyrins and amino acids, have been employed as evidence for the presence of life, in the light of data from experiments related to the abiogenic synthesis of many of these compounds, grave doubts have arisen about the value of such standards. In the beginning of the nineteenth century,

Von Liebig's laboratory at Giessen in 1842, where for the first time students of chemistry were able to do practical work. It was Liebig's friend and pupil Wöhler who made biochemical history by synthesizing urea from inorganic material

the vitalists had argued that molecules containing carbon could arise only from living processes. The work of the early organic chemists showed that this was a very dubious statement. In 1828, Wöhler's synthesis of urea from ammonium cyanate prepared the way for the birth of synthetic organic chemistry.

There are some organic geochemists who contend that petroleum may be abiogenic in origin. The presence of the normal alkanes, porphyrins and other biomolecules would lead one to deduce that the bulk of petroleum has been produced by living matter. However, some of the deposits of hydrocarbons found at Mountsorrel near Leicester, or in the asphalt in Trinidad, do not exhibit the characteristics associated with materials of biological origin. For example, there are no detectable normal alkanes or isoprenoids. On the basis of this criterion alone, one would have to conclude that the hydrocarbons from these different deposits are abiogenic in origin. On the other hand, an examination of the distribution of the different isotopes of carbon (p. 146) hints that some biological splitting-up of the molecules (fractionation) may have taken place. Observations such as these impel one to search for distinguishing marks which would unequivocally tell us whether some molecules were a result of living processes or not.

Specimen of bitumen from Mountsorrel, near Leicester. This and other naturally occurring hydrocarbons do not seem to satisfy all the criteria for a biogenic origin

CARBON ON THE MOON

In the early hours of 21 July 1969, Neil Armstrong crawled out of the spidery-looking vehicle which had traversed over 240,000 miles from Cape Kennedy to the Sea of Tranquillity. He unveiled a plaque which commemorated man's first excursion into an alien world. During the hours of activity which followed, the astronauts collected the precious cargo of lunar dust and rock, eagerly awaited by a multitude of scientists throughout the world. In these samples brought back to earth may be hidden the answers to many questions which have been raised about the origin of the solar system, and about life itself. About 150 selected investigators participated in the exciting exercise of examining the first samples from the moon. The studies ranged from physical measurements of samples to chemical and isotope analysis, and the search for organic compounds related to life processes.

Perhaps one of the most intriguing aspects of the study of the lunar material related to the question of the possible presence of organic compounds. In the study of chemical evolution, an attempt has been made to retrace the path by which life may have appeared on earth. The earth is the model

Opposite: part of the far side of the moon, photographed by the Apollo 8 mission from a height of 70 miles

The Sea of Tranquillity, photo-graphed from the lunar module as the Apollo 11 mission orbited the moon

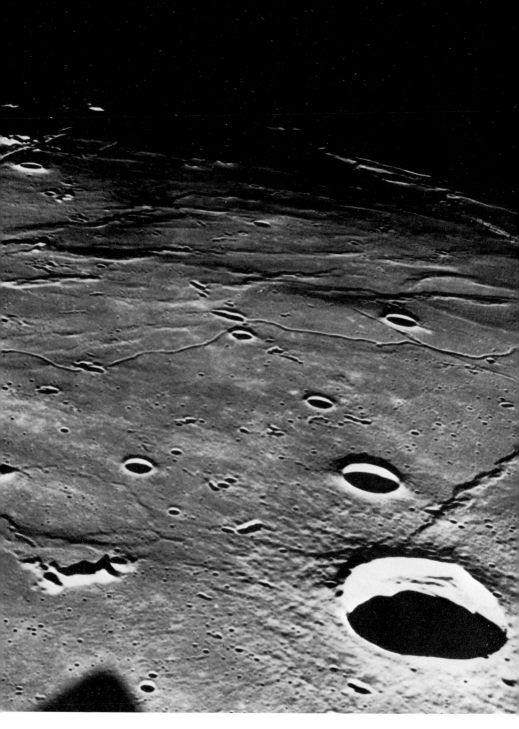

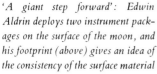

'A giant step forward': Edwin Aldrin deploys two instrument packages on the surface of the moon, and his footprint (above) gives an idea of the consistency of the surface material

laboratory in which we observe first-hand the events which may also be taking place elsewhere in the universe. In the synthetic approach, we have endeavoured to recreate the basic chemical components of life. In the analytical method, we traced our steps backwards through geological time to the very early period when life first began.

From our study of the Precambrian era, it appears that the chances of discovering any rocks older than three billion years are remote. Even in the unlikely event that some sediments are found going back to the first half-billion years of the earth's existence, the possibility of any organic compounds surviving the ravages of greedy microorganisms is virtually nil. Once started, life is notoriously destructive.

Organic matter, which may have been abundant in the prebiotic soup of the early era, would have been used up by the swarms of microbes which were nurtured in the primordial oceans. On the other hand, the rocks and sediments of the lunar soil, from the Sea of Tranquillity, have provided us with samples which may give some clues to prebiotic organic synthesis in the solar system.

The study of the lunar samples is a logical extension of our analytical work on the ancient sediments of the earth. What we are attempting to do is to retrace the path by which cosmic carbon gradually led to the beginnings of life, and eventually gave rise to the biosphere as we know it today. We have indeed come a long way from the vitalistic origin of molecules related to life. Not only do we know that organic compounds can be synthesized without living processes, but also that the very compounds necessary for life can be formed by abiogenic methods.

The moon, together with the planets, is believed to have been formed about $4\frac{1}{2}$ billion years ago from the solar nebula, and dating of the material from the Sea of Tranquillity has upheld this contention. Theories of the evolution of the solar system imply that the moon may have passed very rapidly through a sequence of reducing atmospheres which enveloped it during, and soon after, its origin. Like the earth, the moon must have had a secondary atmosphere, due to emission of gases from the crust, which it lost to space very early in the course of its evolution. The gravitational force of the moon must have been too small to hold these gases captive for long periods of time.

The forms of energy that were regarded as necessary for the synthesis of organic compounds on the earth must have been equally effective on the lunar surface. Ultraviolet radiation, electrical discharges, heat, ionizing radiation – all must have played their part. On the basis of the energy available, many attempts have been made to calculate the amount of organic matter which may have been synthesized on the lunar surface. Since most of this material must have rained down on the moon during the time it was still being formed, it is obvious that the bulk of it must be buried at great depths below the lunar surface. The molecules which would have been produced during the secondary lunar atmosphere may have had a better chance of surviving, provided they were protected from solar radiation, micrometeorite bombardment, cosmic ray influx, meteorite impact, and surface changes which may have taken place over billions of years.

Examining moon rocks

In the expectation of finding molecules related to life or living processes in the lunar samples, several experimenters have examined the dust and rocks brought back to earth by the Apollo astronauts. A large group of scientists, including micropaleontologists, organic chemists, geochemists and mass spectrometrists have combined their talents to analyze these precious specimens.

When the samples first arrived in Houston and were quarantined in the Lunar Receiving Laboratory, certain tests were conducted. These were essentially time-dependent, and had to be performed immediately in case the information that was sought might be lost after exposure to the terrestrial environment. These included biological tests, some microbiological studies, petrographic and geochemical analysis, and other measurements that would detect the presence of short-lived radionuclides.

During the quarantine period, preliminary

The eagerly awaited first samples of lunar rocks (opposite, above) include spherical glassy tektites probably resulting from the intense heat caused by meteorite impact. The same rocks (opposite, below), embedded in plastic, sectioned and polished, show many features familiar to terrestrial geologists

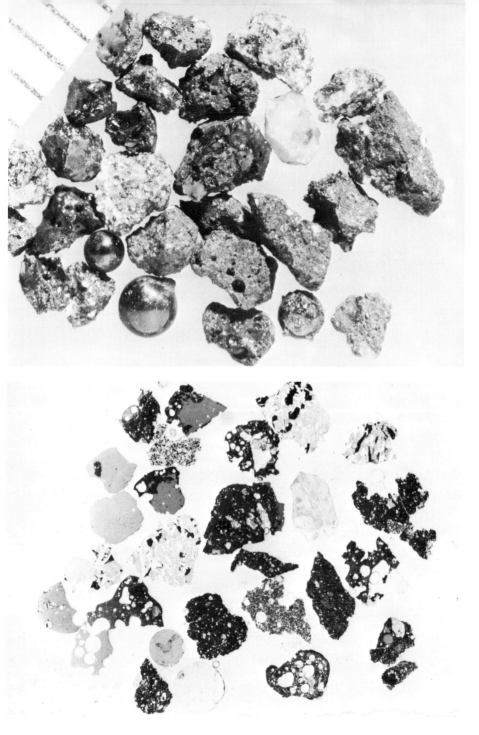

observations were made on the presence of organic matter in the lunar sample. Using an extremely sensitive detector, a small sample was pyrolyzed in a current of hydrogen. The resulting fragments of organic products were swept into the hydrogen flame where variation in intensity was recorded as a measure of the organic content.

Several representative specimens of lunar dust were examined. The total organic carbon was in the range of about 10 parts per million. In parallel experiments, a small amount of the material was placed in a nickel capsule and transferred to the inlet system of the mass spectrometer. The sample was heated from ambient temperature to approximately 500° C. The levels of organic matter observed by this technique were extremely low, from about 0.4 to 5 parts per million. Undoubtedly, these initial results were very discouraging. However, most of the investigators were of the opinion that even if a small amount of organic matter could be found, it was still worth while to pursue the question further and establish the true nature of the carbon in the lunar materials.

One of the biggest problems the organic geochemist faces in precise analytical work of this type is contamination. Advanced methods of gas chromatography, combined with mass spectrometry, have refined our tools to such an extent that we are now in a position to identify the nature and quantity of molecules in terms of parts per billion. However, the art of infra-microanalysis is fraught with unexpected pitfalls. Traces of organic matter from the atmosphere, from solvents, and from the experimenter himself may obscure the results. Ultra-clean laboratories have to be set up for this type of analysis. Filtered air prevents the introduction of any airborne particles. All solvents have to be redistilled and examined for

In the examination of lunar material much effort has been devoted to the search for any sign of biological activity, past or present. Among other experiments, plants have been kept in contact with lunar rocks in a sterile nitrogen-filled chamber. In comparison with control plants (left), tissue changes – possibly due to trace elements – have been noted, but nothing that unambiguously says 'biological activity'

traces of hydrocarbons and amino acids. A complex routine for rinsing of glassware minimizes introduction of any extraneous dust or grit. Rigorous procedures have to be used in all the handling.

With this care and precision, the background levels in the laboratory for the commonly occurring compounds of potential biological significance were well below one part in a billion. This is of particular importance in the analysis of meteorites as a suspicion of contamination has often detracted from the value of many significant findings. A single thumbprint on a glass vessel can give rise to many of the common amino acids found in proteins!

The total amount of carbon was measured by outgassing the lunar sample at about 150° C. at a pressure of less than 1 micron. The carbon dioxide evolved could be measured when the sample was burned at 1,000° C. These values ranged from 140 to 200 micrograms (millionths of a gram) per gram. The most consistent value obtained was 140 micrograms, suggesting that part of the 200 may have been due to contamination from the rocket exhaust. The amount of organic carbon in this material was determined by pulverizing a small amount of it in an atmosphere of hydrogen and helium. The figures give us approximately 40 micrograms per gram, in general agreement with the figure reported in the early analysis from the Lunar Receiving Laboratory.

Since the rocks and lunar dust exhibited an extremely low carbon content, there seemed to be scant possibility that the moon had evolved any life forms during the course of its history. This conclusion was confirmed by careful examination of the surface of the rocks for microstructures. Thin sections were also cut, and examined by light and electron microscopy, but no structures were found which could be interpreted as biological in origin.

In the analysis of compounds containing carbon, it has been found that the two stable isotopes, carbon-12 and carbon-13, can be separated by means of various chemical or physical processes.

The terrestrial ratio for carbon-12 to carbon-13 is about 90 to 1. (This ratio, which is useful for finding out whether some differentiation of organic or inorganic carbon has taken place, is generally measured with reference to a standard mineral; it can be obtained by burning the carbon to carbon dioxide, and measuring the ratio of the two isotopes with a mass spectrometer.) Generally, for extraterrestrial samples such as meteorites, this value is in the region of -4 to -20, while the figure obtained for the lunar material was $+20$. This is considered to be unusually high. At this moment, it is difficult to find an explanation for this heavy carbon content. It is possible that the light carbon may have been lost owing to the continuous action of the solar wind. The protons may have combined with the carbon and, preferentially, with the lighter carbon. The gases formed may have escaped into space.

Organic compounds

A search was also made for those organic compounds present in the lunar sample which could be extracted by various solvents. The scheme used is illustrated in the accompanying figure. This table summarizes the wealth of analytical knowledge that has been gained in many laboratories from analysis of geochemical samples over the years. The sample is first examined for the presence of any material which would fall under the general class of lipids. The solvent used for this extraction is a mixture of benzene and methanol. Any straight-chain hydrocarbons or normal alkanes, branched-chain or isoprenoids, and fatty acids could be extracted by this process. After treatment with benzene-methanol, the sample could be dried and then extracted with water to remove any possible carbohydrates or amino acids which might be present as individual molecules, unbound to each other or to the inorganic matrix. Subsequent treatment with acid would enable release of the constituents of the nucleic acid or the protein molecule.

Although modern techniques available in the laboratory, such as gas chromatography combined with mass spectrometry, could get down to a billionth of a gram, there was no evidence for the presence of any normal alkanes, aromatic hydrocarbons, fatty acids, any of the common amino acids, or the constituents of the nucleic acid molecule. It seemed reasonable therefore to expect that the carbon which was detected in the initial examination would be present in the form of carbides. When the sample was treated with acid, some hydrocarbons were formed, confirming this possibility. The examination of the Apollo 11 samples from the Sea of Tranquillity led us to the conclusion that the concentration of organic matter was about 150 micrograms per gram. The bulk of this sample of carbon was present as unextractable organic matter. Carbides appeared to be present up to about 20 parts per million. The isotope fractionation has given the highest value of the heavy isotope found in any sample of terrestrial or cosmic origin. There seemed to be no evidence for those organic molecules which we have looked for as related to life.

This chart shows the planned lines of analysis to establish whether any organic compounds (see bottom line) were present in the lunar samples. So sensitive are modern laboratory techniques that as little as 150 parts per million of carbon could be found

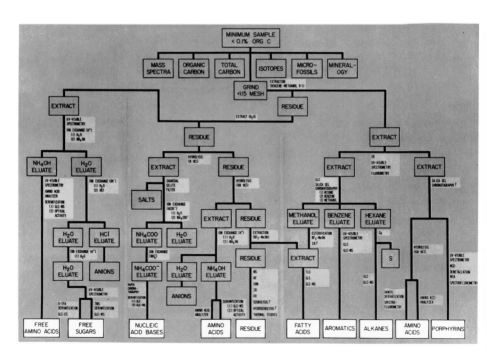

Later Apollo missions

What has been described about the Apollo 11 samples could be applied to the Apollo 12. The total amount of carbon appeared to be approximately the same. There was no indication of any of the organic molecules such as the amino acids, the nucleic acid bases, or the hydrocarbons. On the Apollo 12 mission, the astronauts landed from the Lunar Exploratory Module, and so were able to move away from the contamination produced by the exhaust from the LEM. Samples were brought back which did not show any of the terrestrial contaminations. However, there was no evidence of any organic compounds originating from the moon.

Apollo 11 and 12 samples came from the Maria (lunar 'seas'). These Maria consist of parts of the

A core sample brought back by Apollo 12 shows the fine-grained texture of the soil of the maria, pounded by aeons of micrometeorite bombardment

An Apollo 12 astronaut holds a
container of lunar material while his
companion (reflected in his visor)
photographs him. Right: rocks of all
sizes, down to small pebbles, photographed where they lay on the moon's
surface

lunar soil which had been broken down by continuous micrometeorite bombardment over a long period of time. Under these circumstances, it would be difficult to expect that the carbon-carbon bonds would have survived the intense ultraviolet radiation from the sun and the drastic treatment received by meteorite impact. It is not surprising, therefore, that no evidence for these organic compounds was found in the surface material from the moon. There was some hope that on further missions, when samples were brought back from the highlands, material would be obtained which would have given us some evidence of the early organic chemical history of the moon.

The Apollo 14 mission which, on 31 January 1971, took off from Cape Kennedy and landed on the Fra Mauro highlands, brought back to earth samples which may be truly representative of the primordial crust of the moon. However, here again the preliminary results tell us that the total carbon content is about the same as in the Apollo 11 and Apollo 12 samples. Further, the analysis of a variety of rocks has also given the interesting correlation that carbon and neon appeared to be comparable in abundance. This finding suggests that the carbon that has been detected is only of solar origin, and probably a result of cosmic rays. The solar radiation, especially the particle radiation, accumulates large numbers of charged particles on the surface of the moon, and the carbon there may be nothing else but solar carbon.

In order to detect some of the organic compounds synthesized during the early history of the moon, we may have to go several hundred metres deeper into the crust, where the material may be preserved for us. So far, we have sampled only three locations on the moon, the Sea of Tranquillity, the Ocean of Storms and the Fra Mauro Highlands. Further

Top: a rock sample from the Apollo 12 mission. The surface can be seen to be pitted, and heavily coated with glass. Above: a thin section of an Apollo 12 rock sample (somewhat enlarged) shows a crystalline arrangement which is quite common in volcanic rocks on earth. Above, right: very small samples of lunar rock are vaporized in this apparatus, by radio-frequency induction heating, and the products analysed – one of the many tests carried out by a multitude of scientists throughout the world

exploration is imperative before we can be absolutely certain about the presence or absence of organic matter on the moon. The Apollo 15 astronauts are back with us after their extensive exploration of the lunar Apennines overlooking Hadley Rille. With the aid of a surface drill, a core sample about ten feet in depth has been secured. At the time of writing, we are eagerly awaiting these latest treasures of lunar exploration. Although the search for molecules of biological significance in the lunar sample has, so far, been disappointing, great hopes have been raised about the possibility of finding these precursors of life in the course of planetary evolution elsewhere in our solar system.

The arrow marks the spot, by a bend in the Hadley Rille, where the Apollo 15 mission touched down; it was photographed from the orbiting command module. The rough ground to the right is the Apennine mountains, of which a closer view is shown (left) with the 'moon-buggy' in the foreground

Meteorites provide us with an unusual opportunity of examining organic compounds of extraterrestrial origin. Before the lunar landings, and the return of samples from the moon, meteorites were the only samples of cosmic matter we could take in our hands. About eight hundred of them have reached the earth. Of special interest to the student of the origin of life are the stones known as carbonaceous chondrites, which comprise only a small percentage of all the known meteorites. They are so called because they contain many chondrules, or small rounded bodies, within their masses, and a variable quantity – $2\frac{1}{2}$ per cent to 5 per cent – of organic compounds.

Among the most celebrated of the carbonaceous chondrites is the Orgueil meteorite, which fell in the south of France in 1864. About twenty stones, the largest about the size of a man's head, were scattered over an area of about two square miles near the village of Orgueil, in the department of Tarn et Garonne. About 12 kilograms were recovered soon after the fall, and over 9 kilograms are retained in the Museum of Natural History in Paris.

Part of the Murchison meteorite. This visitor from outer space is now on exhibition at the U.S. National Museum in Washington.

In the western hemisphere, we have the Murray which fell in the state of Kentucky on 20 September 1950. The morning after the event, several stones about 13 kilograms in weight were recovered. Most of the Murray is in the U.S. National Museum in Washington. The Lancé fell in France, in the Loir et Cher department on 23 July 1872. About 4 to 6 kilograms were recovered; the largest stone is preserved in the Museum of Natural History in Vienna. More recently, in Mexico, we had the Allende. A giant fireball exploded near Pueblito de Allende in Chihuahua, Mexico, on 9 February 1960. Large masses have been recovered, and several studies have been made. Most of this material is now in the U.S. Natural History Museum in Washington.

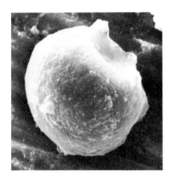

This small rounded body (about a hundredth of a millimetre across) is from the Orgueil meteorite. A three-dimensional enlargement in the scanning electron microscope gives it a structure and surface texture very like those of certain cells

The presence of organic material in carbonaceous chondrites has long been known. As long ago as 1834, the Swedish chemist Jöns Jakob Berzelius, working at the Karolinska Institute in Stockholm, published his analysis of the Alais chondrite, which had fallen in France in 1806. Most of the Alais appeared to be composed of clay minerals. Berzelius claimed that by extracting a specimen with water, and by a process of distillation, he had obtained complex substances. This analysis, which began over 140 years ago, ushered in the intensive study of organic compounds in carbonaceous chondrites which is being pursued once again today with the most advanced analytical techniques available to us. Another classic meteorite analysis was that done by Wöhler in 1859. He extracted a piece of the Kaba meteorite with alcohol, and identified organic substances which appeared to be similar to humic acid in character.

After the fall of the Orgueil meteorite on 14 May 1864, many chemists decided to take a look at fragments of extraterrestrial matter thus made

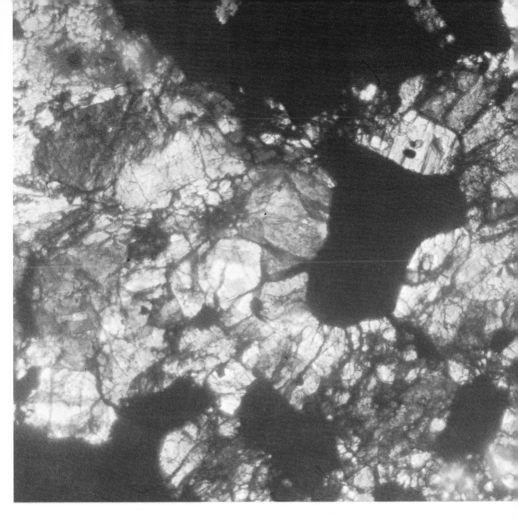

available to them. Daubrée, for example, obtained some of the stones immediately after the fall and, after making quite sure that the contamination from the soil had been removed, he began to analyze it in collaboration with Cloez. In his first report, made public in 1864, he stated that carbon was present in the interior of these stones. He also noted that there was a salt, containing ammonium and chlorine, probably ammonium chloride, which had gradually accumulated on the fused crust owing to the emission of gases from the inside of

Magnified thin section of a carbonaceous chondrite. These bodies contain small quantities of organic compounds from space

the stone. According to Cloez, there was 6.4 per cent of organic matter resembling humic acid in this meteorite. This observation is in close agreement with the value found by Wiik in 1956. Four years after the fall of the Orgueil meteorite, Berthelot made quite a thorough study of it, and stated that there were carbon compounds of the general formula C_nH_{2n+2}, suggesting that he had isolated some hydrocarbons similar to the normal alkanes.

Since the analysis of the Alais, Kaba, and Orgueil meteorites in the last century, there was very little effort to make a further study of them till the middle of the 1950's, when George Muller, at Birkbeck College, University of London, made an extraction from the South African Cold Bokkeveld meteorite and examined the organic matter present in it. Since that time, there has been a great resurgence of activity in the analysis of carbonaceous chondrites. Hydrocarbons have been found in them, and amino acids, purines, and pyrimidines have been claimed to be present. However, as the problem of contamination is inevitable in meteorite studies, many of the results reported have been regarded with scepticism.

The Apollo programme stimulated an unprecedented development of techniques for the analysis of organic matter in the lunar samples. The precise methods of gas chromatography, combined with mass spectrometry, gave unequivocal evidence for the presence of various organic compounds in a meteorite. The techniques by which the left-handed and right-handed amino acids could be separated also enabled the analyst to establish whether some of the organic compounds present in these meteorites were truly of extraterrestrial origin. If the mixture of organic compounds found resembled those which were generally produced

$10\,\mu$

In examining extra-terrestrial matter, whether moon rocks or meteorites, contamination has always to be considered a possibility. This drawing was published as a possible alga-like form (from the Orgueil meteorite) but it is now regarded sceptically

abiogenically in laboratory-designed experiments, there might be some reason to believe that they were not contaminants. In the case of the amino acids, the left-handedness, or the right-handedness, of these molecules provides intrinsic criteria for the separation of the earthly from the extraterrestrial amino acids.

Fresh evidence

While the study of organic matter in meteorites was in the doldrums, an event took place which rekindled interest in this field. On Sunday 28 September 1969, around 11 a.m., a flash was seen across the noonday sky near Murchison, a small town about 85 miles north of Melbourne, Australia. The fall was witnessed by many people, and there were several who were able to give a reliable account of the event. The sighting was recorded in Mildura, about 256 miles north-west of Murchison. An eyewitness from Canberra, 230 miles to the east, described the appearance of a flashing light which slowly descended from the sky. At Bayswater, 76 miles south of Murchison, a bright object was reported which appeared to glow with yellow colours, moving downward at a very steep angle. At the closest point of sighting, the town of Kialla West, about 17 miles north of Murchison, there was a report of a bright orange ball with a silver rim and dull orange conical tail leaving a blue smoke trail, which lasted about one or two minutes. Over Murchison, this object in the sky exploded, and fragments rained to the ground. There were many people who heard the fall. The noise lasted almost a minute. There was a report like thunder or sonic booms.

Immediately after this meteorite fell, eyewitnesses assembled on the scene. Some reported that they had noticed something like the smell of pyridine or methanol. This was strongly suggestive of the presence of organic matter. The total weight of material collected was about 82 kilograms, and most of it is now in the Australian Museum, the U.S. National Museum in Washington, and the Field Museum of Natural History in Chicago.

The availability of a freshly fallen meteorite minimized the possibility of terrestrial contamination. Our laboratory was fortunate enough to receive a piece of the Murchison, soon after its fall, through the efforts of Carleton Moore of the Institute of Meteoritics, State University of Arizona. A small stone was obtained with a fusion crust around it. This crust was carefully removed, and an interior piece of the meteorite was taken, crushed, and extracted with water. It was then extracted for hydrocarbons and finally hydrolyzed for the presence of amino acids. Our analysis very clearly showed that there were hydrocarbons present in the meteorite, but the gas chromatographic pattern seemed to imply that they were abiogenic in character. The examination of the amino acids revealed that those present in the meteorite appeared as both forms, the left-handed and the right-handed. This could not be due to contamination. Further, it was apparent that there were a number of amino acids which are not commonly found in proteins. These too could not be ascribed to terrestrial sources, and had, therefore, to be indigenous to the meteorite.

A further study of the extract of the organic matter of this carbonaceous chondrite showed us that the isotope ratio was very different from what is normally found in organic matter upon the earth. The meteorite appeared to be enriched with a heavy isotope of carbon, further confirming its cosmic credentials. The analytical procedures used by us have established unequivocally that this meteorite had six amino acids commonly found in protein, and twelve that do not occur in natural protein. All those amino acids which have an asymmetric carbon atom or, in other words, could appear as left-handed or right-handed molecules, were found in equal amounts.

It must be admitted that there is a distinct possibility of terrestrial contamination in meteorite analysis. However, recent biological contamination would invariably lead to the predominance of the left-handed molecules which are commonly found in earth organisms. The identification of the non-protein amino acids would also strongly argue against contamination.

The question arises, where do the extraterrestrial amino acids come from? One possible explanation is that these amino acids were, perhaps, present at some period in the meteorite in either left-handed or right-handed form, and then were converted into the racemic ('both-handed') form during the course of time. The possibility that an extra-terrestrial organism could have had either the left-handed or the right-handed form cannot be discounted. But, if we take an earthly view, it would be difficult to explain the presence of the non-protein amino acids. The production of one form or the other by a non-biological process would also appear to be unlikely. As we have already seen, in spite of extensive experimentation, there is no clear evidence why an abiotic process would produce one form rather than the other. We are therefore led to believe that the amino acids in the Murchison meteorite were produced by an abiotic extraterrestrial process.

The analysis of this meteorite thus provides us with, perhaps, the first conclusive evidence for the process of chemical evolution occurring elsewhere in the universe.

*Jupiter. The great red spot, about
30,000 miles long, is prominent at
top left*

The hypothesis of chemical evolution states that the molecules necessary for life could have been formed from various energy forces acting upon the raw material which was in the earth's primordial atmosphere. It has been tacitly assumed that if similar conditions prevailed elsewhere in the universe, the same sequence of events would have taken place.

The planet Jupiter is an object of intense study. Its present atmosphere of methane, ammonia, hydrogen, and water may be considered similar to that of the primitive earth. Spectroscopic evidence has shown very clearly that these molecules, which probably were part of the early solar nebula, are being held by gravitational forces in the Jovian atmosphere. The largest of the giant planets, Jupiter is the most massive in the solar system, and is twice as heavy as all the other planets put together.

A superficial consideration might prompt one to

How the evidence is collected. These three spectra (in the near infra-red range) are of the sun (top), Jupiter and ammonia gas. The close correspondence between the last two shows the presence of ammonia in Jupiter's atmosphere

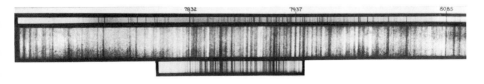

7832   7937   8085

dismiss the possibility that any form of life, or the precursors of life, could ever appear on a planet so far removed from the sun. It is nearly 500,000,000 miles away from the sun, five times as distant from the sun as the earth. But recent astrophysical studies have disclosed that though the outside of Jupiter is a cold and frigid sheath of ammonia crystals, beneath this frozen layer is a boiling inferno of liquid and gas. The greenhouse effect, produced by the release of heat during the melting of ice and solid ammonia, gives rise to higher temperatures. Immediately below the clouds is a layer of liquid ammonia droplets followed by a region in which gaseous ammonia is predominant. Water, in the form of ice, liquid and vapour, occupies the domain below the ammonia. High temperatures and pressures prevail close to the metallic surface of solid hydrogen. The calculations of the two astrophysicists, Peebles and Gallet, heightened our interest in Jupiter. The raw material and energy essential for making the molecules of life abound within the expanse of this colossal planet.

The red spot

Opposite: an experiment in the author's laboratory simulated reactions possible in Jupiter's methane-rich atmosphere. An electric discharge passed through a mixture of methane and ammonia produced, after a time, several precursors of biologically important compounds as well as an orange-red translucent polymer, which would possibly explain the colour of the red spot. Recently a spectral absorption feature observed in this material was found in the spectra of Jupiter, suggesting that this experiment was on the right lines

Another source of great interest is the enormous red spot on Jupiter. This has been observed by astronomers for generations, and remained an enigma to them. Some have explained it in terms of a giant body afloat in a Jovian ocean. Others have considered the presence of frozen free radicals which are generated by different kinds of energy. The chemical suggestions, however, seem to be more plausible since, ultimately, a satisfactory explanation has to be propounded at the molecular level. It is possible that the present atmosphere of the Jovian planet could, on the action of various forms of energy, give rise to molecules which are themselves dark-red in colour.

At the Ames Research Center, we have used a stainless steel electric discharge chamber as a reaction vessel. A cold finger within this reactor was maintained at the temperature of liquid nitrogen and acted as a surface at which some of the organic matter synthesized could be deposited. Four windows enabled one to observe the progress of the experiment. The feed line supplied the mixture of gases and, at the same time, acted as one of the two high-energy electrodes. The cold finger, carrying the liquid nitrogen, acted as a second electrode. The polymer formed was deposited on the walls of the stainless steel vessel.

Other experiments were conducted at room temperature in a glass vessel containing methane and ammonia. The results of these investigations were encouraging. When the gases formed were examined by mass spectrometry, hydrogen cyanide was identified. This molecule is essential for prebiological synthesis. Its appearance in experiments simulating primitive earth conditions has been well-documented (p. 80). Its presence in comets has been inferred from spectroscopic studies, and, more recently, radio astronomers have given us evidence of its presence in the interstellar medium.

Acetylene is synthesized along with hydrogen cyanide. Its high-energy triple bond confers on it a unique capacity to undergo further reactions giving rise to aromatic ring structures. This build-up of acetylene also suggests that higher polymers could be made by this method. Give the organic chemist hydrogen cyanide and acetylene, and with these building blocks he could create a wide range of organic molecules which may be of utmost significance for biological processes.

Gas chromatography and mass spectrometry were used to analyze the volatile materials produced in the Jovian simulation experiments. Several nitriles, including glycinonitrile and propionitrile, were found. Glycinonitrile is the precursor of glycine, the simplest of the amino acids, and the one most easily generated in abiogenic synthesis. The higher homologues of these nitriles can be regarded as the forerunners of other amino acids.

In our search for a possible explanation of the red colours of the planet Jupiter, which, incidentally, may be the same colours appearing on the planets Saturn and Uranus, we concentrated our efforts on the examination of the polymer produced from methane and ammonia. It is a ruby-red material of high molecular weight, soluble in methanol, giving a transparently bright red solution. This brightly coloured material may have the composition of a complex mixture of polynitriles.

Reproducing the red colour in a laboratory exercise is no demonstration that this is, indeed, the material on the planet Jupiter. However, before long, we will have an opportunity of confirming these observations by a direct look at the planet. With our giant telescopes and with our high-flying aircraft equipped with devices to analyze the reflected light from the planet, it may be possible to search for the presence of some of the spectral lines exhibited by the synthesized material.

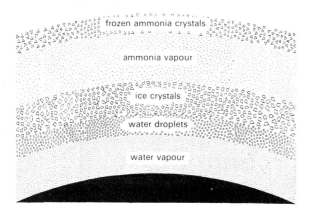

frozen ammonia crystals

ammonia vapour

ice crystals

water droplets

water vapour

Cross-section of the Jovian atmosphere, as revealed by spectroscopy. This is probably very like the primitive (pre-oxygen) atmosphere of the earth

A restricted Grand Tour of the planets is now planned for later this decade, when many of the planets of our solar system will be aligned in a position realized only once in 179 years, and may provide a welcome opportunity for the study of the giant planets. A single spacecraft may be directed to fly by Jupiter and between Saturn and its rings, and send data back to us. The use of probes, which may be aimed at the planet, holds promise for future exploration of Jupiter. A mass spectrometer may be employed to analyze the Jovian atmosphere as the probe enters the planet at the red spot.

Jupiter appears to be a repository of a large amount of organic matter which could be utilized in the evolutionary processes leading to life. The red spot may be a window to the whole of the inside of Jupiter, coloured red on account of the presence of some prebiological organic molecules.

Artist's conception of the route to be taken by an unmanned spacecraft on a 'grand tour' of the solar system

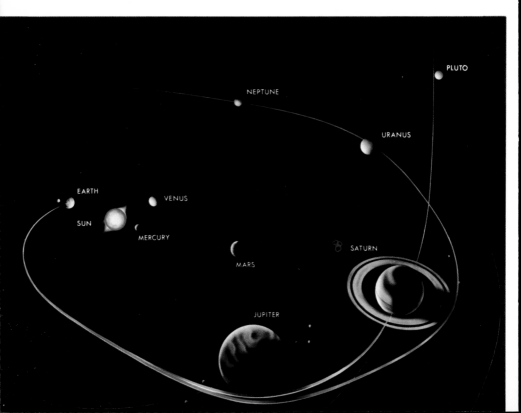

MARS, A POSSIBLE ABODE OF LIFE

The search for extraterrestrial life has been defined as the prime goal of space biology. Such a discovery may influence human thinking far more profoundly than the Darwinian or Copernican revolutions. If our sallies into space establish that Martian life is a reality and its origin independent of life on earth, we cannot then escape the conclusion that there is nothing unique about the origin of life on earth and that the interplay of cosmic forces would have given rise to a similar sequence of events in the countless number of planetary systems in the universe.

In our quest for life beyond the earth, three possibilities exist. The first aspect to be considered is the landing of instruments, or man, somewhere in the universe. Our present state of knowledge and technology would undoubtedly restrict this to our own planetary system, at least for the time being. A second route would be via radio contact with civilizations in outer space. As we shall see later, this presupposes the existence of intelligent beings beyond the earth with a technology as advanced as, or even superior to, our own. Lastly, there is the experimental aspect of the problem. Here, the retracing in the laboratory of the path by which life

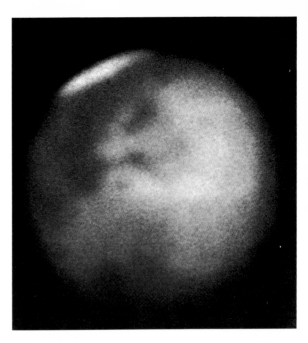

Mars: two views 12 hours apart, showing changes due either to rotation or to dust storms in the thin Martian atmosphere

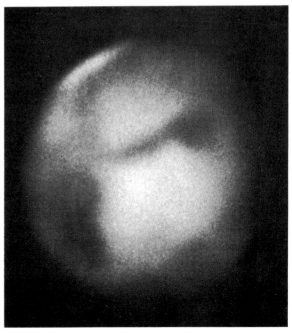

may have appeared on the earth might provide convincing proof of its existence elsewhere in the cosmos.

Our effort to land an instrument or, eventually, a scientist-astronaut on a neighbouring planet, is primarily directed to the planet Mars. The possibility of life there has often been raised. Its canal-like structures and the seasonal wave of darkening which crossed the planet has fostered the assumption that there must be some life on Mars. Some have postulated the existence of highly intelligent beings who, by incredible feats of engineering, have saved for themselves the depleting water supply on the planet. These speculations have fired the imagination of the planetary scientist and made him determined to answer the question: Is there life on Mars?

When we leave speculation aside, and consider

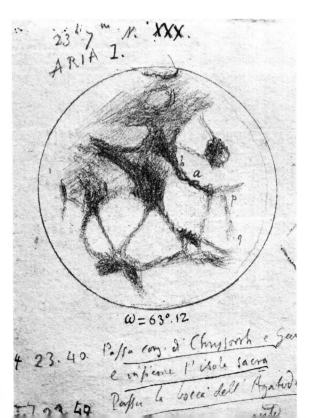

The Italian astronomer Schiaparelli, in 1879, made this sketch of what he guessed to be 'canali' (channels) on Mars. Hence the misunderstanding about 'canals' and the speculations about Martian engineering

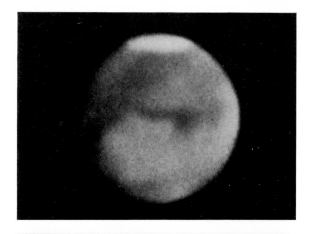

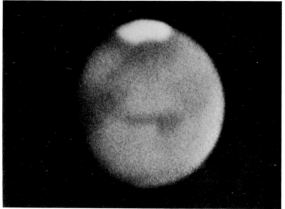

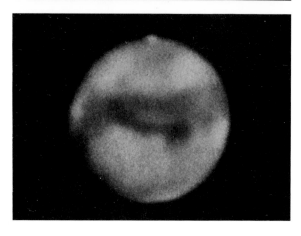

Regular observation of Mars shows white polar caps, probably composed of frozen carbon dioxide, which wax and wane with the seasons. The dark markings, too, show seasonal changes. Right, top to bottom: mid-April, mid-May, early August (in the Martian year)

the actual conditions that prevail on Mars today, we must, most likely, exclude the existence of advanced forms of life. However, the physical conditions are such that low forms of life, microorganisms for example, could survive. As Mars has been the object of astronomical observation for generations, its gross characteristics are well known. Its distance from the sun is approximately 140 million miles. The diameter is about one-half that of the earth, and its mass is about one-tenth the earth's. Its period of rotation is almost that of the earth, 24 hours and 37 minutes. A glance at Mars on photographs available to us through the giant telescopes and from spacecraft shows that there are polar caps which are white in colour. Originally, they were thought to consist of water, and they seemed to wax and wane with the seasons. It was believed, at one time, that the dark areas increased in size when the polar caps became smaller. Recent evidence attests to the fact that the polar caps are composed primarily of carbon dioxide. Although the dark areas – which cover about a quarter of the surface of the planet – also change in size, the previous explanation that this was a result of the growth of vegetation is no longer tenable. In spite of all this, we are still at a loss to interpret the nature of this variation in the dark areas of the planet. There is also a third region, rather bright, almost reddish in colour, which has been called the desert area. The average temperature is about $50°$ colder on Mars than on the earth. On the Martian equator, the temperature rises to about $30°$ C., which is the temperature on the earth on a warm day.

A proper understanding of the nature of the Martian atmosphere is indispensable in considering Mars as a candidate for life. The total atmospheric pressure is about 6.5 millibars. This is less than a hundredth of the pressure of the earth's atmosphere.

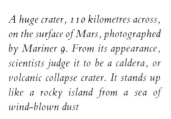

A huge crater, 110 kilometres across, on the surface of Mars, photographed by Mariner 9. From its appearance, scientists judge it to be a caldera, or volcanic collapse crater. It stands up like a rocky island from a sea of wind-blown dust

Since the mountains of Mars may rise to as much as 14 kilometres in height, it might be argued that the pressure on the surface varies from 3 to about 15 millibars. Its atmosphere consists of carbon dioxide, carbon monoxide and water vapour, with carbon dioxide emerging as the major constituent. Small amounts of carbon monoxide, and traces of oxygen, are present. No nitrogen has been detected.

There is a heavy ultraviolet flux on the Martian surface. Since there is no ozone shield to afford protection from the short-wavelength ultraviolet light, radiation at the lower end of the spectrum at about 1900 Angstrom units may be reaching the

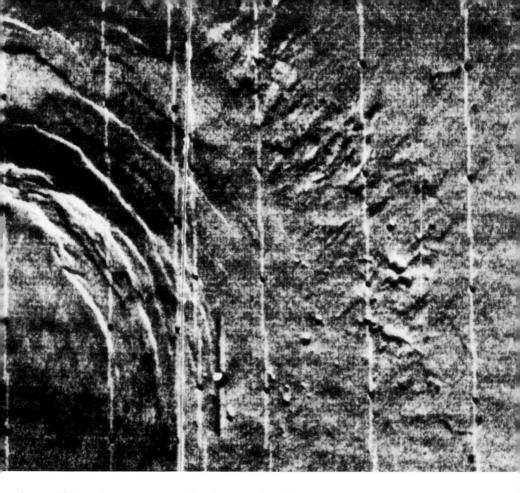

planet. Although water vapour has been noticed in the atmosphere, this is extremely low – about 15 to 20 microns – only about a thousandth of the amount of water present in the earth's atmosphere. There is no evidence of any liquid water on Mars.

So far, only a small portion of the topography of Mars has been photographed, but in 1972, a spacecraft in orbit around Mars will photograph practically two-thirds of the planet.

The size and distribution of the craters on Mars were a great surprise to the planetologist when they were first photographed during the Mariner Missions. There were indications that these features were as old as the red planet itself. If this contention can be substantiated, we may have to infer that Mars is probably very similar to the moon. At present, however, there is very little information in favour of this hypothesis.

The conditions on Mars imply that the prospects for life are extremely bleak. However, the possibility of life cannot be ruled out completely. On the basis of its size and distance from the sun, the early history of Mars may have been similar to that of the earth. It may have contained an atmosphere which was denser than the present one. Chemical evolution may have taken place on the planet and proceeded apace. If the early conditions had been favourable, biological evolution would have flourished. In such a process, adaptable organisms would have overcome many obstacles placed in the way of their development. Therefore, by analogy to terrestrial life, it is not unreasonable to suppose that the evolutionary process would have selected those organisms which had been able to resist the severe conditions of the Martian environment: the rigours of dehydration, the scarcity of water, the high incidence of lethal ultraviolet fluxes, and the vagaries of the freeze-thaw cycles.

The limiting factor for life on Mars may be the unavailability of water. Future investigations will attempt to answer this question. There may be water beneath the surface as a permafrost layer. Local areas of thermal activity might make liquid water available close to the surface. The 1972 fly-by is eagerly awaited to provide further information on the physical parameters of the planet.

Tests and experiments

Ever since the possibility arose that a spacecraft could be landed on Mars, much thought has been given to the kind of experiments that should be

In this laboratory at the Ames Research Center, California (left), scientists have simulated conditions to be expected on Mars – including cycles of frost and thaw – and found that certain Earth micro-organisms can survive and even reproduce in such conditions. In the insulated chamber (above) is a red soil containing iron oxide, which is very like the observed Martian surface

included. During the last two years, several teams have been appointed by the National Aeronautics and Space Administration to formulate experiments which might furnish useful information in our search for life on Mars. The test for organic compounds would probably most easily fulfil the requirements for simplicity and sensitivity. While the absence of organic matter on Mars might have to be regarded as eliminating the possibility of life, its presence would not necessarily imply that there *is* life on the planet. Any organic compounds found might be either a result of meteoritic impact, since Mars is close to the asteroid belt and might receive a greater share of meteorites than does the earth, or they might be the result of early prebiological synthesis. Since relatively little is known about the stability of organic compounds over long periods of time, a great deal of uncertainty would surround experiments of this type.

Another investigation which could be under-

The Mariner spacecraft that orbited Mars in 1971. Narrow- and wide-angle television cameras can be seen below the spacecraft, which was powered by solar cells in the wing-like panels. From wing-tip to wing-tip it measured a little over 22 feet

taken would be to detect the metabolic activity of organisms in Martian samples. Heat production, the evolution of gases, and the variation in the pH could be measured. In contrast to chemical analysis, these determinations would have to be made at intervals in order to look for changes in the observations. In these preparations, there is a temptation to use a large number of substances which might stimulate metabolic activity. For example, the addition of water or organic matter could activate dormant or resting organisms into increased activity. In the absence of such additions, the energy utilization by any organisms in the sample could be so low as to escape notice. On the other hand, the addition of any extraneous agent might inhibit, rather than stimulate, metabolic activity. A useful test may thus be destroyed; it may be a case of over-kill.

Such uncertainties may also be related to experiments designed to identify specific enzymes. It has long been thought that biochemical techniques could provide a wealth of information regarding the organisms which may be present on the planet. If the Martian organisms are microorganisms, and it is most likely that that would be the case if they were found, techniques would have to be devised to use automated microscopic scanning of soil samples. The essential point which seems to emerge is that there is no single unequivocal test for the presence of living organisms. Single tests are bound to be ambiguous.

The Viking mission, scheduled for 1975, is an attempt to assemble a large number of different techniques for the search for life on Mars. Twelve scientific teams were selected for this mission: for imaging, water mapping, and thermal mapping; for spectrometric and molecular analysis, meteorology, the physical parameters, biology, magnetic

properties, and atmospheric studies. Three of them have a direct bearing on the question of life on Mars – the imaging, molecular analysis, and biology teams. The purpose of the imaging and molecular investigation is to characterize the landing site and provide biologically relevant data. Two cameras will be used, and each of these will be capable of viewing virtually the entire area accessible to the surface sampler. The molecular analysis group will take samples of the Martian surface and subsequently examine them for organic content by vaporizing some of the material into a high-efficiency gas

Opposite: Artist's conception of the landing manoeuvre, from orbit to the Martian surface, planned for the mid 1970's. Commands for the final manoeuvres, such as parachute opening and firing of the retro-rockets, will be part of the orbiting spacecraft's program. Below: Model of the 'Viking' instrument package designed to touch down on the surface of Mars about 1976. Its prime goal will be the search for signs of life

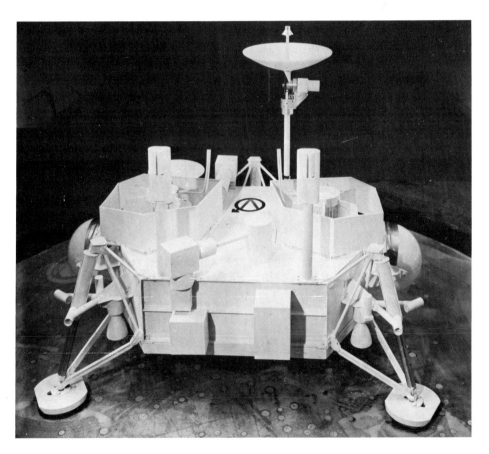

181

chromatographic column which, in turn, will be connected to a fast-scan mass spectrometer. If any organic compounds are present in the Martian soil, the fragments observed by the mass spectrometer will enable them to be characterized.

'Direct biology' experiments would consist of four different types of analysis on portions of the same sample of Martian soil. These samples will be taken after first scanning the local environment. The samples will be simultaneously scanned by molecular analysis techniques. In one experiment, only water vapour will be added. In the other, in addition to the water, some organic matter will be supplied to encourage any latent metabolic activity.

The fixation of radioactivity of carbon dioxide, or carbon monoxide, into organic compounds will be determined to provide evidence of biological activity. A soil sample will be incubated in the light together with the native Martian atmosphere, which has been augmented by the addition of a trace of radioactive gas. The unreacted gas can be flushed out of the soil sample. The residual carbon dioxide will then pass through a copper oxide coated firebrick column, which retains organic compounds. The radioactivity detector will be used to monitor the effluent from this column. In a further experiment, a sample of soil, together with water, will be used for optical measurements. This solid, together with the liquid, will be incubated in the Martian atmosphere. The scattering of light through this solution will be monitored. If microorganisms grow in this solution, there will be a change in the turbidity of the once-clear liquid. This change in turbidity would be an indication of the growth of organisms on the planet.

In a related experiment, a sample of the Martian soil will be moistened with an aqueous solution containing a dilute mixture of organic compounds

labelled with carbon-14. This mixture is once again enclosed in a very small volume, together with some of the Martian atmosphere. If there are any microorganisms in the soil, they could possibly utilize the radioactive material that is presented to them in the form of carbohydrates or amino acids. The release of any gaseous radioactive compounds could be monitored. Once again, the presence of radioactivity in the atmosphere above the sample would be an indication of biological activity.

In yet another attempt to establish the presence of growth, or change, in the organic composition of the Martian soil, the sample will be wetted with a mixture of nonradioactive organic compounds. At various intervals, the atmosphere about it will be sampled by gas chromatography. Indication of any biological change could be obtained by studying the composition of the gas in the space above the

One of the experiments of the Viking mission is likely to be an automatic sampling of the soil. One early idea, depicted here but now superseded, involved ejection of sticky cords from an instrument capsule, which would then be drawn in again for analysis of any fragments adhering to them.

incubation chamber. All these experiments are planned at a temperature of approximately 10° C. If one, or other, produces a positive signal, the result would prove that microorganisms are present. However, in order to run a control on these results, the whole series of experiments will be repeated after the Martian soil is sterilized at 160° C for about three hours. This would eliminate any kind of living organism, and provide a much-needed control.

The programme planned for 1975 is, in a sense, a precursor of future missions. Ultimately, men will go to the planets; we shall never be satisfied with instrumental life detectors alone. If the results from our instruments are negative, we shall be doubtful of them. If the answer is positive, the urgency for man to go to Mars will be even greater. However, from a scientific point of view it is important that we obtain as much information as we can about possible life forms before men come into direct contact with this planet. The moment a man lands on a planet, it becomes contaminated. While it is possible to sterilize all the equipment involved, it may be impossible to ensure that the planet will not be infected by earthly organisms when man sets foot on Mars. Necessary precautions should also be taken to prevent contamination of the earth by potentially pathogenic Martian organisms. The safest course would be to first obtain pertinent biological information by the use of one-way missions.

Apart from the earth in our solar system, only the Martian surface may be in a position to sustain living organisms. Yet all that we know about the planet from ground-based observations, from fly-bys, and orbiting satellites, establishes that the conditions on Mars are extremely harsh by terrestrial standards. Water is in very short supply.

If bodies of water were never present on the surface, the probability of finding life on Mars is meagre. Despite these uncertainties, and the immense technical difficulties involved in trying to reach Mars, it is a challenging venture from the scientific viewpoint. The information that we can obtain from the study of Martian organisms, if they exist, will be of momentous consequence. On earth, living organisms, while exhibiting a vast variety and diversity in size and form, are fundamentally alike. Their chemical composition is very similar. It is a basic premise of the hypothesis of chemical evolution that all terrestrial types may have been derived from a single ancestor. However, the question that is completely obscure and that may never be solved by our earthbound studies, is whether this similarity is a result of some fortuitous biological accident occurring early in the course of evolution, or whether it is dictated by the intrinsic properties of the elements and molecules of living matter. If organisms are found on some other planet, and if they have properties uniquely different from those we know on earth, the horizons of biology would be immeasurably broadened.

Biology today has only one subject matter – life on earth. We would be able to extend its frame of reference to life beyond the earth. If, on the other hand, the life we discover on Mars is very similar to life on the earth, we will be faced once again with the question of whether life arose on the earth or whether it was brought to earth from another source. The hypothesis of panspermia suggested by Arrhenius might receive a new lease of life.

The planet Mars has physical characteristics which do not exclude life. However, if life, even in its most rudimentary form, is not detected there, we might be compelled to modify some of our concepts of chemical evolution.

Astronomers are in general agreement that life must be of common occurrence in the universe. Their calculations enable one to assume that intelligent life must have evolved in a large number of sites beyond the earth. An estimate of this distribution, made by several astronomers, puts the figure at about a million in our own galaxy. The distance between these 'civilizations' may be as much as one thousand light years. By human standards, of course, the separations are almost infinite. 'There is one race of men; one race of gods; both have birth from a single mother, but sundered power holds us divided, so that one is nothing, while for the other the brazen sky is established as their citadel for ever', wrote Pindar in the sixth Nemean ode.

In trying to establish the number of communicative civilizations in the cosmos, attempts have been made to relate various parameters which might give us some idea of their distribution. A communicative civilization might be defined as one having a technology significantly enough advanced as to permit the detection of another civilization over interstellar distances.

From 98,000 miles, viewed from the Apollo 11 spacecraft, the Earth shows no obvious signs of intelligent life. The picture shows part of Europe and almost all of Africa

Several years ago, a group of astronomers came together to discuss the fascinating topic of talking to other intelligent beings, somewhere in outer space. Some of their findings can be summarized in the following formula for the number of communicative civilizations:

$$N = R_* f_p \, n_e f_e f_l f_c \, L$$

R_* = the mean rate of star formation
f_p = the fraction of stars with planetary systems
n_e = mean number of planets in each planetary system with the conditions suitable for the origin and evolution of life
f_e = the fraction of planets on which life can actually develop
f_l = fraction of life-bearing planets on which intelligent life has evolved
f_c = fraction of planets bearing intelligent life which can give rise to a communicative civilization
L = lifetime of a technical civilization

Astronomers have given various numbers to these functions. Of these figures, only R_* is well known from stellar and astro-physical statistics. The estimates of the other figures are based on unproven theories and observations which may be regarded as merely speculative. The biological parameters are also subject to a great deal of variation. Some of the early steps in chemical evolution have been retraced but we have not yet been able to establish the presence of life anywhere else other than on the earth. In considering all these figures, we are most in the dark about the value of L. Some of the factors which might cause a fluctuation in L might be nuclear war, a cosmic catastrophe, or even loss of interest in science and technology. The appraisal of this number will generally be dependent on the

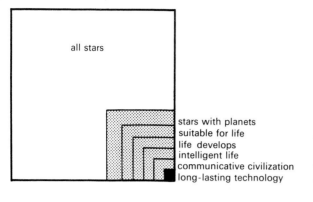

all stars

stars with planets
suitable for life
life develops
intelligent life
communicative civilization
long-lasting technology

How many counterparts to ourselves, intelligent and able to communicate, could there be in the universe? However conservatively one estimates the parameters, the answer could be of the order of one thousand possibilities in our Galaxy alone. And that is one galaxy among a hundred thousand million

subjective state of the individual making it. Conversely, we might consider situations in which L is enhanced. These may be the regeneration of a communicative species on a planet after destruction or, perhaps, invasion by intelligent beings from another solar system. In such an event, L might have a much larger figure. Calculations made by Sagan and Drake suggest that the number of communicative civilizations in the galaxy would be about a thousand and that the minimum distance between these would be about a thousand light years.

Effective means of communication are imperative in order to reach distances of one thousand light years. Some guess may be hazarded about the possible methods of communication. Interstellar rocketry is one possibility. The relativistic effects could cause rocket designs for near-light velocities to be almost beyond the technology of the next thousand years. A tentative solution has been presented in the form of Buzzard's ram jet, in which the propulsion fuel would be gathered from the interstellar medium in the course of the flight. However, the low density of any material in space might set limits to such a possibility. Travel of this

LIFE BEYOND THE EARTH

Looking towards the centre of the Milky Way, this star cloud in the constellation Sagittarius gives a graphic notion of the enormous number of stars in just one galaxy – any two of them separated by a distance measured in light-years. Intelligent life there must certainly be, somewhere in that immensity – but how to communicate with it?

type would become feasible only if we are willing to assume that civilizations are extremely altruistic and are willing to wait thousands of years for celestial visitors.

Nuclear particle radiation which can carry information with the speed of light is another likelihood. All the known useful nuclear particles present far more energy than photons, but the information content is similar. A third probability is electro-magnetic radiation, which can travel at the speed of light, with little interference, over a thousand light-years or more. Useful signals containing a significant amount of information can be delivered at a cost which appears very reasonable even today. This would be the most effective and economical means available to us, and would probably be the best one to use in the present circumstances.

If electromagnetic radiation is chosen as the method of solving our problem, the next question is the best wavelength at which to transmit a message. This was first discussed theoretically by Coconni and Morrison, who speculated that the optimum frequency for transmission would be that of the hydrogen line at twenty-one centimetres. The subharmonics and harmonics of the hydrogen line have also been suggested as possible candidates. One search for intelligent life has already been made on this frequency, which has been regarded as the one that intelligent beings elsewhere in space might use – presumably because transmission at frequencies of lower wavelength will be distorted by natural radio noise.

Frank Drake has compared this monumental search for intelligent beings in the universe to meeting a friend in New York City without making arrangements in advance about a rendezvous. One does not roam the streets looking everywhere. The most likely places in which to look are those that are already familiar, Grand Central Station, for example, or Times Square. There are similar places in every city, with which most people are acquainted. This is what the radio-astronomer is in search of – a Grand Central Station of the galaxy – some special frequency about which everyone in the Milky Way would be aware. This, indeed, is the emanation of the hydrogen line.

Focusing on the nearest stars is apparently the best mode of seeking for intelligent signals in the light of our present state of knowledge. The two nearest that fall in this category are Tau Ceti, in the constellation of Cetus, and Epsilon Eridani, in the constellation of Eridanus. Both these are about ten light-years away. In the search conducted at the Greenbank Observatory, each morning at three o'clock, the telescope was pointed to Tau Ceti. When Tau Ceti set beyond the mountains, the telescope was directed towards Epsilon Eridani, and the search was carried on. A signal was picked up twice, the same signal each time. This was an exciting event but, on moving the antenna, it was obvious that these were actually signals from the earth and not from space. At the end of two months, no evidence of signals from space could be found on the records. These were the first steps in the endeavour of the National Astronomical Observatory in 'Project Ozma'.

Clearly, one should not be disappointed, or discouraged, because the first attempts of 'Project Ozma' (named after the mythical princess of Oz) to find another civilization were not more fortunate. It will take many long years, with large radio telescopes and more sensitive receivers, to achieve any degree of success.

Let us assume that after years of futile listening we receive a particular series of pulses from beyond our

solar system. The message is repeated every 22 hours and 53 minutes – presumably the mean length of our callers' day. The pulse occurs in integral multiples of a minimum separation. Writing ones for pulses, and filling the blanks with appropriate numbers of zeros, we get the binary series shown below, consisting of 1,271 ones and zeros. 1,271 is the product of two prime numbers, 31 and 41. This strongly suggests that we arrange the message in a 31 by 41 array. When we do so, putting blanks for zeros and a circle for each pulse, we get the non-random pattern shown at the foot of the page.

Opposite: the Howard E. Tatel radio-telescope at Greenbank, West Virginia, used in a systematic but so far fruitless search for signals from space

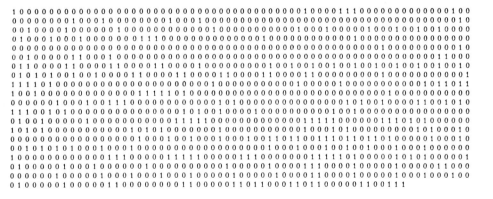

```
1 0 0 0 0 0 0 0 0 0 0 0 0 0 0 0 0 0 0 0 0 0 0 0 0 0 0 0 0 0 0 0 0 0 0 0 0 0 0 0 1 0 0 0 0 1 1 1 0 0 0 0 0 0 0 0 0 0 0 0 0 0 1 0 0
0 0 0 0 0 0 0 0 1 0 0 0 1 0 0 0 0 0 0 0 1 0 0 0 1 0 0 0 0 0 0 0 0 0 0 0 0 0 0 0 0 0 0 0 0 0 0 0 0 0 0 0 0 0 0 0 0 0 0 0 0 0 1 0
0 0 1 0 0 0 0 1 0 0 0 0 0 0 1 0 0 0 0 0 0 0 0 0 0 1 0 0 0 0 0 0 0 0 0 1 0 0 0 1 0 0 0 0 0 1 0 0 0 1 0 0 1 0 0 1 0 0 0 0
0 1 0 0 0 1 0 0 0 1 0 0 0 0 0 0 0 1 1 1 0 0 0 0 0 0 0 0 0 0 0 0 0 0 1 0 0 0 0 0 0 0 0 0 0 0 0 0 0 1 0 0 0 0 0 0 0 0 0 0 0 0 0 0 0
0 0 0 0 0 0 0 0 0 0 0 0 0 0 0 0 0 0 0 0 0 0 0 0 0 0 0 0 0 0 0 0 0 0 0 0 0 0 0 0 0 0 0 0 0 0 0 0 1 0 0 0 0 0 0 0 0 0 0 1 0
0 0 1 0 0 0 0 0 1 1 0 0 0 1 0 0 0 0 0 0 0 0 0 0 0 0 0 0 0 0 0 0 0 0 0 0 0 0 0 0 0 0 0 0 0 0 0 0 0 0 0 0 0 0 0 0 0 1 1 0 0 0
0 1 1 0 0 0 0 1 1 0 0 0 0 1 0 0 0 0 1 1 0 0 0 1 0 0 0 0 0 0 0 0 0 1 0 0 1 0 0 1 0 0 1 0 0 1 0 0 1 0 0 1 0 0 1 0 0 1 0 0 1 0
0 1 0 1 0 1 0 0 1 0 0 1 0 0 1 0 0 0 1 1 0 0 0 1 1 0 0 0 0 1 1 0 0 0 0 1 1 0 0 0 0 1 1 0 0 0 0 0 0 0 0 0 1 0 0 0 0 0 0 0 0 0 1
1 1 1 1 0 1 0 0 0 0 0 0 0 0 0 0 0 0 0 0 0 0 0 0 0 0 1 0 0 0 0 0 0 0 0 0 0 0 1 0 0 0 0 0 1 0 0 0 0 0 0 0 0 0 0 1 0 1 1 0 1 1
1 0 0 1 0 0 0 0 0 0 0 0 0 0 0 0 0 1 1 1 1 1 0 1 0 0 0 0 0 0 0 0 0 0 0 0 0 0 0 0 0 0 0 0 0 0 1 0 0 0 0 0 0 0 0 0 0
0 0 0 0 0 0 1 0 0 0 1 0 0 1 1 1 0 0 0 0 0 0 0 0 1 0 1 0 0 0 0 0 0 0 0 0 0 0 1 0 1 0 0 1 0 0 0 0 1 1 0 0 1 0 1 0
1 1 1 0 0 1 0 1 0 0 0 0 0 0 0 0 0 0 0 0 1 0 1 0 0 1 0 0 0 0 1 0 0 0 0 0 0 0 0 0 1 0 0 1 0 0 0 0 0 0 0 0 0 0 0 0 0 0
0 1 0 0 1 0 0 0 0 1 0 0 0 0 0 0 0 0 0 0 1 1 1 1 0 0 0 0 0 0 0 0 0 0 0 1 1 1 1 0 0 0 0 0 0 0 1 1 0 1 0 1 0 0 0 0 0 0
1 0 1 0 1 0 0 0 0 0 0 0 1 0 1 0 1 0 0 0 0 0 1 0 0 0 0 0 0 0 0 0 0 0 0 0 1 0 1 0 0 0 0 0 0 0 0 0 1 0 1 0 0 0 1 0
0 0 0 0 0 0 0 0 0 0 0 0 0 0 0 1 0 0 0 1 0 0 0 1 0 0 0 1 0 0 0 1 0 0 1 1 0 1 1 0 0 1 1 1 0 1 1 0 1 1 0 1 0 0 0 0 0 1 0 0 0 1 0
0 0 1 0 1 0 1 0 1 0 0 0 1 0 0 0 1 0 0 0 0 0 0 0 0 0 0 0 0 0 0 1 0 0 0 1 0 0 0 1 0 0 0 1 0 0 0 1 0 0 0 1 0 0 0 0 0
1 0 0 0 0 0 0 0 0 0 1 1 1 0 0 0 0 0 1 1 1 1 1 0 0 0 0 0 1 1 1 0 0 0 0 0 0 0 1 1 1 1 1 0 1 0 0 0 0 0 0 1 0 1 0 1 0 0 0 0 0 1
0 1 0 0 0 0 0 1 0 0 0 1 0 0 0 0 0 0 1 0 0 0 0 0 0 0 0 0 0 1 0 0 0 0 0 1 0 0 0 0 1 1 1 0 0 0 0 1 0 0 0 0 0 1 0 0 0 0 0 1 1 0 0 0
0 0 0 0 0 0 1 0 0 0 0 0 1 0 0 0 1 0 0 0 1 0 0 0 1 0 0 0 1 0 0 0 0 0 1 0 0 0 0 0 1 0 0 0 0 1 1 0 0 0 0 1 0 0 0 0 0 1 0 0 0 1 0 0 0 1 0 0
0 1 0 0 0 0 0 1 0 0 0 0 0 1 1 0 0 0 0 0 0 0 0 1 1 0 0 0 0 0 1 1 0 1 1 0 0 0 1 1 0 1 1 0 0 0 0 0 1 1 0 0 1 1 1
```

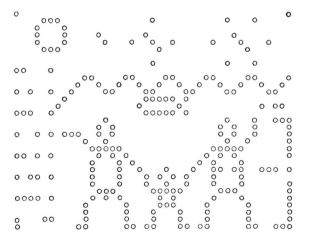

Information about the senders of this imaginary 'message from outer space' could be quite surprisingly full – their physical appearance, reproduction, solar system, basic chemistry. This is all conveyed by a single succession of 'on-off' pulses of radiation at 21 cms wavelength

Apparently, we are in touch with a race of erect bipeds who reproduce sexually. There is even a hint that they might be mammals. The crude circle and column of dots on the left is a clue to their sun and planetary systems, including the fourth planet, which is evidently their home. The wavy line over the third planet indicates that it is covered with water. The fishlike form shows that there is marine life there. The bipeds know this, so they must have space travel. The diagram at the top will be recognized as the symbols for hydrogen, carbon, and oxygen, denoting that their life is based on carbohydrate chemistry. Finally, the vertical line at the lower right suggests that the figure is eleven units tall. Since a wavelength of twenty-one centimetres, on which we received the message, is the only measure known to both of us, we conclude that their beings are 231 centimetres, or seven feet, in height. Thus, despite the fact that we have no common language, we have been able to communicate a great deal of information to each other.

It is interesting to note that a recent Russian publication has called attention to several Biblical incidents which, they suspect, reflect possible contact with extraterrestrial civilizations. For example, the events narrated in the Slavonic Enoch are considered to be an account of a visit to earth by extraterrestrial cosmonauts. In this particular context, there are other legends which deserve serious study. One of these is the Babylonian account of the founding of the Sumerian civilization by the Apkallu, who were supposed to be representatives of an advanced, non-human, and possibly extraterrestrial society.

There is little reason to doubt that we shall rediscover, one by one, the essential conditions which once determined, and directed, the course of chemical evolution. Our sallies into space with man at the helm, or with robot engines, will give us a better understanding of our own solar system. Verbal communications with our brothers in distant galaxies might unfold to us knowledge of a true cosmic biology. We may even reproduce the intermediate steps to life in the laboratory. Looking back on the biochemical understanding gained during the span of one human generation, we have the right to be judiciously optimistic. In contrast to unconscious nature, which had to expend billions of years in the process of creation, conscious nature has a purpose and knows the outcome.

The sun god Shamash rising from behind the mountains: Babylonian cylinder seal, c. 2250 BC. Could this and similar legends have been inspired by extraterrestrial visitors?

GLOSSARY

aldehyde: hydrocarbon derivative containing the group H—C=O, for example acetaldehyde CH_3CHO.

alkane (normal): a hydrocarbon, derived from petroleum, of the general formula C_nH_{2n+2}, having an open chain of carbon atoms; the first four members are gases, the higher members liquids, and those above 16 carbon atoms are waxy solids.

anaerobic: living or active in the absence of free oxygen; a class of bacteria which are inhibited or killed by free atmospheric oxygen.

aromatic: containing one or more benzene rings.

autotroph: an organism capable of self-nourishment: can use simple inorganic carbon and nitrogen compounds as its sole source of food.

biosphere: that part of the world in which life can exist; it includes parts of the earth's crust, oceans and atmosphere.

biota: living organisms of a particular place or period.

dissociation: reversible splitting of a molecule into simpler units, such as smaller molecules, atoms, or ions.

fatty acid: organic acid of the general formula $C_nH_{2n}O_2$. Examples are acetic acid CH_3COOH and stearic acid $C_{17}H_{35}COOH$.

heterotroph: an organism which is unable to use simple inorganic substances for food.

hydrocarbons: compounds consisting solely of carbon and hydrogen. They may be in straight or branched chains, or in rings.

hydrolysis: chemical change produced by inter-action of a compound with water, resulting gener-ally in the addition of the elements of water.

isoprenoid: a compound based upon the isoprene structure C_5H_8. These include many naturally occurring materials such as rubber and cholesterol. In organic geochemistry pristane and phytane are important isoprenoids.

lipid: name given to a group of organic substances including fats and esters with analogous properties. Examples: fatty acids, soaps, waxes.

morphology: the science of the outward form and inner structure and development of animals and plants.

nitrile: an organic compound containing the cyanogen grouping (CN), a precursor of an amino acid.

photochemical: refers to the effect of light in causing or modifying chemical changes.

photosynthesis: the natural process by means of which carbon dioxide and water are converted into carbohydrates in growing plants with the aid of sunlight.

racemic: optically inactive, that is to say unable to rotate a plane of polarized light. Describes a mixture of equal amounts of levo- and dextro-rotatory compounds.

radiation: energy in forms such as light, heat, X-rays or electricity, which is transmitted by electromagnetic waves.

radical: a fundamental constituent of a chemical compound that remains unchanged during a series of reactions. Examples of radicals are such groups as OH, CN, SO_4 and NO_3.

reducing: causing the state of an atom or compound to become more negative owing to a gain of one or more electrons by the atom. Reducing conditions are those under which excess hydrogen is present.

reflux: condensed vapour returned to and allowed to flow down from the top of the fractionating column in counter current to the rising vapours.

tetramer: a molecule formed by the union of four identical simpler molecules. For instance, C_8H_8 is a tetramer of C_2H_2.

vitalism: the doctrine that the functions of a living organism are due to a vital principle distinct from physiochemical forces.

BIBLIOGRAPHY

Bernal, J. D., *The Physical Basis of Life*. London, 1951

— *The Origin of Life*. London, 1967

Bivet, R., and C. Ponnamperuma (eds.), *Molecular Evolution I* (Proceedings of the Third International Conference on the Origin of Life, held at Pont-à-Mounan, France, in April 1970. Amsterdam, 1971

Calvin, M., *Chemical Evolution*. New York, 1969

Monod, J., *Chance and Necessity* (transl. Austryn Wainhouse). New York, 1971

Oparin, A. I., *Genesis and Evolutionary Development of Life* (transl. Eleanor Maass). New York, 1968

Pittendrigh, S., W. Vishniac and J. P. T. Pearman (eds.), *Biology and the Exploration of Mars*. Washington, D.C., 1966

Ponnamperuma, C. (ed.), *Exobiology*. Amsterdam, 1972

Schroedinger, Erwin, *What is Life?* Cambridge, 1944, New York, 1956

Shapley, Harlow, *Of Stars and Men*. Boston, Mass., 1950, London, 1958

Shklovskii, I. S., and Carl Sagan, *Intelligent Life in the Universe*. San Francisco, 1968

Teilhard de Chardin, Pierre, *The Phenomenon of Man* (transl. Bernard Wall). London and New York, 1959

Thomas, J. André (ed.), *Biogenèse*. Paris, 1967

LIST AND SOURCES OF ILLUSTRATIONS

The diagrams were drawn by Elizabeth Winson

INDEX *Numbers in italics refer to illustrations*

Huxley, Thomas Henry 23–4
hydrocarbons 102, *133*, 135
    in experiments 66, 71
    in extraterrestrial samples 131–2, 147–9,
        158, 160
hydrogen 39, 41–5, *50*, 63, 80–1, 113–14,
    146, 163, 196
    solid 164
hydrogen bonding 35
hydrogen cyanide 48, 76, 80, 90–2, 166
hydrogen flame test 143
hydrogen-ion concentration (pH) 38–9
hydrogen line 192–3
hydrogen sulphide 39
hydrolysis 91–2, 131, 160
hypersonic energy 59–60, 71

Iceland *56–8*
illite 83
inert gas 113
intelligent life beyond earth 169, 171,
    187–97
interstellar medium 48–9, 80, 82–3, 189
interstellar rocketry 189
ionization patterns *70*
ionizing radiation 51, 54–5, 58, 66–7, 78,
    80, 142
ions 51, 113
iron 41, 113
    meteoritic *43*
iron bacteria *127*
isoprenoids 132, 134–5, 147
isotopes 135, 137, 146, 148, 160

Jeans, Sir James 30
Jupiter, 32, 42, *162*, 163–8
    simulation experiments 166–7

Kaba meteorite 156, 158
Kakabekia umbellata 126, 127
Kant, Immanuel 30
kaolinite 83
Kennedy, Cape 137, 151
Khorana, H. G. 89
Kilauea volcano, Hawaii 55

Krueger 60 double star *28*

Lactic acid *106*
lagoons 25, 58, 76, 87–8, *89*
Lancé meteorite 156
Laplace, Pierre de 30
lava 55, 68
Leeuwenhoek, Antony van *15*, 16
leucine 90
Lichtenberg figure 70
Liebig, Justus von, laboratory *134*
life, definition of 36–9
    building blocks of 24, 71, 85, 118, 166
    early organisms 29, 45–7, 121–30, 140–1
    see also extraterrestrial life
light 45–7, 68, 167
lightning *52–3*, 65, 66
light years 187, 189, 192–3
linear accelerator 66, *67*, 80
lipids 102, 132, 147
lithium fluoride 68
Lucretius 14
lunar dust 137, 142–3, 146
lunar exploration *136*, 137–53
Lunar Exploratory Module 149
lunar highlands 151–2, *153*
Lunar Receiving Laboratory 142, 146
lunar samples 143, *145*, *148–50, 152*
    analysis of 142–8
lunar 'seas' (Maria) 149
lunar surface *140*, 141–2, *150*, 151
lysine 36

Macromolecules 25–6, 39, 87, 95, 99, 116
magnesium 39, 41, 113
magnetic field of earth 108
manganese 113
Maria, lunar 'seas' 149
Mariner Missions 174–5, *178*
Mars 28, 32, 169–85, *170, 171, 172*, 174–5
    'canals' 171
    craters *174–5*
    dark areas 173
    dehydration 176
    polar caps *172*, 173